I have taught Adult Education classes, given workshops, and have facilitated the RCIA (Rite of Christian Initiation of Adults) process for many years and in a variety of cultures. There are classes that offer ways of understanding the scriptures through studying the historical background of each gospel, the author and audience, etc. Janet offers another format for reflecting on the gospels through the eyes of individuals who encountered Jesus while he lived and taught. This type of reflection is helpful for both individuals and groups to enter into these encounters with Jesus, and then to have one's own conversation with Jesus or one of the other Gospel characters. Too often we approach the gospels intellectually, forgetting that they are narratives, and are meant for readers to enter into them as Janet has done. These letters are great for use in a variety of settings and offer a means for individuals to personalize the gospels, leading into a richer spiritual life.

—Catherine D. Kent, MA

DEAR KATHRYN

A SPIRITUAL JOURNEY THROUGH THE NEW TESTAMENT

BY

JANET GENERA

WingSpan Press

Published in the United States and the United Kingdom
by WingSpan Press, Livermore, CA

The WingSpan name, logo and colophon are the trademarks of
WingSpan Publishing.

ISBN 978-1-59594-998-1 (pbk.)
ISBN 978-1-59594-969-1 (ebk.)

First edition 2020

Printed in the United States of America

www.wingspanpress.com

1 2 3 4 5 6 7 8 9 10

This book is dedicated to Kathryn Kelly with gratefulness for her spiritual, therapeutic direction and support on my journey.

TABLE OF CONTENTS

FOREWORD

I first began working with Janet on December 10, 1997. I was certified as a Spiritual Director through the Order of St. Benedict in 1994 and also licensed as a Professional Counselor that same year. I will be forever grateful for this combination of training in spiritual, mental, and emotional healing. Much of my training through the Order of St. Benedict was in Jungian Psychology and my training as a Professional Counselor was connected deeply with the spiritual realm. My graduate thesis was entitled *Agnes Divinitatis,* or the study of the feminine divine as a therapeutic tool for healing both the masculine and feminine traumas of our lives. Writing that thesis was transformative for me, helping me to delve deeply into my own woundedness and struggles with the societal inequities of our gender and racial biases.

Janet and I worked together for roughly seven years. In that time, working with Janet was both a challenge and a pleasure. She began writing her Dear Kathryn letters early in our time together. She wanted to gain a deeper connection with the characters in the New Testament by identifying with them and sharing their experiences as if she was each individual. These writings reflect both her deep insight and her creativity. When she could not reconcile the purpose or meaning of a passage, she created a beautiful narrative to find her way through the passage and find peace, or even to enter into the pain of the character.

These letters are deeply reflective and intimate examinations of many New Testament characters. I am grateful to have walked

1

with Janet along her spiritual and emotional journey. Her letters are true spiritual treasures.

Please read her letters with both an open heart and an open mind.

Blessings and appreciation,

Kathryn Kelley, M.A., NCC, LPC Spiritual Director, Order of St. Benedict, OSB Kelley Institute of Integrative Therapy, LLC

DEAR READER

My name is Janet Genera. I am a retired RN and former massage therapist and Therapeutic Touch practitioner. I am a divorced woman, mother of five, and a spiritual pilgrim. I am *not* a Bible scholar. I knew very little about the culture or geography of the New Testament era. Most of what I know, I learned from the entertainment media. In fact, for most of my life, I knew little or nothing about the Bible.

I grew up Catholic in a time when reading the Bible by lay people was discouraged, because of fears we might misinterpret it. I went to a Roman Catholic high school and took a yearly religion class, but I remember no Bible studies. All I remember about the classes were the "do not" instructions. The Second Vatican Council changed all that, encouraging Catholics to read the Bible. I tried for years to include Bible reading in my spiritual practices, but I felt no connection to the people or their situations. They were just words in a book, the language stilted, the writing foreign to me.

One day, during a therapy session with Kathryn Kelly, I complained to her, "I just can't get into the Bible." She suggested I write about it. She made no suggestions on how to go about it, but I went home that day and wrote my first Dear Kathryn letter. That was in 1999.

I was as surprised as anyone about the format. I felt moved by the Spirit to assume the personae of various New Testament characters. It came so easily. When I was done writing that first letter, I felt totally immersed in the lives of the characters. I identified with their feelings, joys, and fears. Each character

3

jumped off the pages, letting me become a part of their lives. This has continued, ever since, for every letter I have written.

I envisioned Kathryn as being homebound because of a physical affliction. I saw her as a wise woman, a healer, an intuitive, a person to whom others turned for guidance and support. She was someone with whom they could share their most intimate feelings.

As you read these letters, I hope you can suspend judgment about various facts: that the language sounds like it is written by an American female, that literacy was not common at that time in history, and that, I am sure, there was no Middle East Postal Service. It was never my intent to be historically accurate.

The Spirit did not seem to mind that these letters do not form a history lesson or Bible class. These letters came about in an effort to make the New Testament more personal and relevant to me—which it did. I had been writing these letters for a few years before I began to read books, listen to CDs, and attend classes, all related to the New Testament.

I also stopped writing these letters for several years after Kathryn suggested that I publish them. Fear of failure or ridicule, and/or my pride and ego, were involved in that decision. I always promised myself I would get back to the letters and every few years I would write one or two more.

In 2019, I was given the grace to want to finish them and miraculously met editor Shirin McArthur, who agreed to work with me. My spiritual journey has now brought me to a place of being comfortable in the sharing of these letters, without any expectation from those who read them.

I know the Spirit wanted me to write these letters because I could identify with the characters. The message I received is that I have nothing to fear because I am a beloved daughter of the Divine and sister of Jesus the Christ. My hope is that, in reading these letters, you will immerse yourself in these characters' lives and see their humanity.

If you wish, feel free to use the extra space at the bottom of each letter to document your thoughts, feelings, and any responses to the characters.

I pray they will offer you healing, consolation, and instructive illumination, and as they have for me.

—Janet Genera

THE ANNUNCIATION

Grace and peace to you, dear Kathryn, from your devoted friend Anne.

I hope you are well and that Yahweh continues to bless and protect you. Clearly, your infirmities have never stopped you from making yourself available to anyone who needed your help. You have been such a gift to me and my family whenever the need arose. Each time you counseled us, sharing your wisdom, guidance, and your deep devotion and faith in the God of Israel, it brought deep relief from whatever the issue was at the time. From the youngest to the oldest among us, for all the creatures of the earth, you have been a manifestation of Yahweh's unconditional love and acceptance. You are one of Yahweh's chosen ones.

Well, those prior incidents seem as nothing now in comparison with what has happened in our family. Mary, my good, loving, shy, obedient daughter is with child. I know you must be as shocked and disbelieving as I was when she told me. I would have wagered my life that she was a virgin. My heart feels broken, and I am filled with fear and dread. What will her father do? How will her brothers react? What will our friends and family think?

I have suggested that Mary write to you with news of her pregnancy and I wanted to prepare you. You were of much help to her when she had difficulty reconciling herself to her future physical relationship with her betrothed, Joseph. He agreed to delay intimate relations until she was ready. Both Joseph's parents, as well as Joachim and I, were pleased with the betrothal and looked forward to this union taking place.

Mary came to love Joseph very much for his patience and understanding and was just now getting ready to set a date for the marriage ceremony. All of this makes it even harder to understand how this pregnancy could have happened.

When Mary told me the story of how her pregnancy occurred, I feared for her mental wellbeing. My daughter's child, the Son of the Most High? I know in my heart that Mary is an honest, devout, loving, and kind young woman, but how can any of this be true? I know Mary believes what she is telling me and does not lie, but I cannot believe such a story. I fear for her mental health.

I have tried not to let her know how distressed I am feeling. I do not know what to do. My tears are shed secretly. I do not wish to further add to Mary's stress, as she is not herself, and certainly Joachim will demand to know why I am so upset. How will I tell her father about this change in his chaste, beloved daughter?

I do not know what he will do when he hears of her pregnancy. I do not know what Joseph will do or what his parents will say. What will our family and friends think? I am so frightened, and beside myself with worry. I pray and pray for direction and Yahweh brought your name to mind. In my desperation, I once again turn to you for guidance and prayers.

I feel I must soon tell Joachim and together we can tell Joseph. But I will wait until I hear from you or receive some sign from the Most High.

Shalom and love,

Anne

Dear Kathryn, your faithful friend Anne is filled with joy and peace and hopes the same for you.

Thank you for responding so quickly. It has been two weeks since Mary told me the news of her pregnancy. As soon as I heard from you, I prepared myself to tell Joachim. That evening, I prayed for the courage to share the situation with him, then did so.

When I told him the news, he could not believe it either. I told him she was pregnant, as she has missed two of her monthly bleeding times. He was so hurt, and then became very angry. He wanted to know who the father was—if not Joseph, then who?

I told him the whole impossible story. That night, we wept and prayed together, finally falling asleep in each other's arms after a very long time.

I do not know how long I slept, but when I woke, it was still dark. I had had a most remarkable dream. I dreamt that my mother, God rest her soul, was in my kitchen, preparing food. She asked me why I was so upset and crying. "Stop being so foolish," she said, and told me to accept that our family had been chosen by the Spirit for this great honor. "Did you forget we were of the House of David?"

I lay there for quite a while, thinking about the dream, believing that it was just wishful thinking. Oh, if only it were true! I wanted to wake Joachim to tell him about the dream, but chose to let him sleep.

A short time later, he sat straight up in bed and began shaking me—he thought I was still asleep. Once I responded, he began telling me his dream—and it was the same exact dream I had!

We were both overwhelmed, remorseful for our doubts and joyful in our appreciation of the fulfillment of the prophecy. We now believe the truth of the story with every fiber of our being and we glory in the wonder of God. What we do not know is what is in store for our beloved daughter and our family, but Joachim swears he will take care of Mary and the baby and we have nothing to fear if we put our trust in the Creator.

We will talk to Mary and assure her that she and her child will be well taken care of, no matter what Joseph decides when we speak to him.

You know, Joachim just charges the villagers what they can afford to pay for the bread he bakes, so we have barely enough to meet our needs. He is such a kind and generous man and I will increase my sewing so the extra money I make will provide for Mary and our grandson.

We put our trust in Yahweh and thank you for your prayers and guidance.

Shalom and love,

Anne

Dear Kathryn, grace and peace to you from your faithful friend Sarah, mother of Joseph.

Joseph just told us that Mary is pregnant and he is not the father of the child. We were astounded at the news, as well as disappointed in Mary, though I tried not to show it because Joseph is so devastated. He loves Mary very much and feels betrayed. Since Mary had refused to have sexual relations with him, he is angry that she chose to be with another man. She says there is no other man, but she is pregnant nonetheless.

Because of this, Joseph has been withdrawn and despondent, going through the motions of his life here at home and at his work. You know what a fine carpenter he is, but his work is deteriorating. I hate to see him suffering so. There is nothing I can say or do to relieve his pain.

Joseph does not seek to punish Mary by causing a scandal, but will quietly divorce her. I have yet to talk to Anne and Joachim. They must be devastated as well. The four of us were so looking forward to this union of our children. We loved Mary like a daughter, even before she and Joseph were betrothed.

Also, being a midwife, I was looking forward to delivering my first grandchild. I so love the work I do, preparing the women, attending the birth, and following up until the mother is able to be on her own. I cannot tell you how many times, after the evening meal, Joseph has had to listen to me talk with his father about the delivery that took place that day. I imagine it was not always easy for him to overhear, but he didn't seem to mind and sometimes he even asked questions. It was as important for me to share the experience of my work as it was for my husband to tell me about his day at work.

So yes, I am very disappointed that I will not be delivering what would have been my first grandchild. Mary was a lovely girl, a kind spirit, who brought joy to all she encountered. I do not know why this is happening to our family and how she could have changed so quickly. None of this makes any sense. I cannot even imagine what the gossip will be like when the village finds out about this. Will we all be shunned? I have much fear.

I love Joseph very much. He is such a good man, a good son, and would have been a good husband. It is Mary's loss.

I feel so helpless. If you have any suggestions, please let me know. Please add your prayers to ours so Joseph will be relieved of his suffering.

In Yahweh we trust,

Sarah

Grace and peace to you, from your elated friend Elizabeth.

Kathryn, Kathryn, Kathryn, how I wish you were here to share my joy, my excitement, my anticipation, my wonder, my pleasure. I cannot begin to write down my thoughts and my feelings. I am overcome with the wonder of the Almighty, so very thankful for the benevolence of a kind and loving God!

Are you wondering what has precipitated all of this? Are you thinking, "Get to the point, Elizabeth"? Well prepare yourself: I am pregnant! Pregnant with a son we are to call John. I know you are probably thinking I have lost my mind, but it's true. Even the midwife has confirmed it.

Let me start from the beginning. Zechariah was at the Temple in Jerusalem. It was his turn to be in the Sanctuary, when an angel appeared to him and announced I was to bear a child, a holy child, a child of God who is to lead our people and prepare the way for the Messiah. He is to be called John.

Needless to say, Zechariah was terrified and confused. Because he doubted the angel, he was struck dumb, at least until the birth of the child, he was told. Since that day, he has only been able to share with me by writing.

I thought he had lost his mind. I was very worried about him. He continues to be mute and to write about meeting the angel. So, after several weeks, I called the physician to examine him. He could find no problem or reason Zechariah could not speak. After the doctor heard the whole story, he suggested a midwife examine me, and lo and behold, she found me to be with child. I almost fainted.

You remember the many, many years I prayed and prayed and fasted so the Lord might answer my prayers for a child. At times, I felt a hole so deep in my heart, I thought I might die. I asked the Lord, time and time again, how I had displeased Him, what I had done or not done. But no answer came.

I was so ashamed. I was "Elizabeth the Barren" to all who knew me. They looked at me with pity and wondered what sin I had committed to be so severely punished. There were days I could not get out of bed, could not sleep or eat. I was in torment. Then—a miracle! My dearest friend and cousin, Anne, had a baby, called Mary. I was there to help Anne and care for the baby as she regained her strength. I fell in love with Mary immediately as I held her after the birth. I was with Anne when she had her boys, but this time it was different. It was as if God wanted Mary to have two mothers. Loving, unselfish, caring Anne allowed that to happen.

Having Mary in my life saved my life. I do not know how long I would have lasted without a child to love as my own. Now I will have the honor to carry and bear a child, to love and nourish him as I have loved and nourished Mary. I have a daughter and now I will have a son. I am truly blessed.

I am feeling wonderful; I have never had more energy. My appetite is good and I sleep with the peace of the Lord engulfing me. Zechariah, on the other hand, seems to be distant and withdrawn. It must be very difficult for him to be unable to speak. It must get tiring for him to have to write everything down or gesture to communicate. You know what a worrier he has always been. I cannot seem to ease his mind or give him any comfort at this time.

I know all will be well, and I pray for Zechariah to know this as well. Please make this your prayer as well.

Elizabeth

Dear Kathryn, this is Mary, a faithful and obedient servant of Yahweh.

I am writing this letter as instructed by the angel Gabriel.

I wanted to write to you before you heard the news through the grapevine. I am pregnant. I know it is hard to believe. It's hard to believe it myself, since I have never been with a man.

Let me tell you the whole story. As you know, when Joseph and I were betrothed on my 15th birthday, I kept putting off having relations with him. I came to see you because I was very afraid and anxious. I was not ready for that part of our relationship. We live in the same town, but I did not know Joseph very well. He is quite a few years older than me and there were very few opportunities to get to know one another.

Upon your advice, I finally told him I was not ready to have a physical relationship with him. He said that was fine and we should take some time to get acquainted. We met once a week at your suggestion and we feel more comfortable with each other. He was very patient, kind, and attentive to me during that time. I began to admire him for the man he is: strong, competent, wise. He's always taking time to help both his family and mine when needed. He never pressured me, but said I was worth the wait.

All that happened because of your advice and support and again I thank you from the bottom of my heart.

Then, about two months ago, I woke from a sound sleep to see a man in the room. He was surrounded by bright light. I thought I was dreaming.

The man spoke and said he was the angel Gabriel, sent by God. Then I was sure I was dreaming. He continued to speak to me and I was terrified. He said, "Be not afraid, you are with child." I was confused and very frightened. I knew none of this could be true and told him so. "You are to bear the Son of Man," he said. I was to call the baby Jesus. "You are special in the eyes of God," he said. Then the angel simply disappeared.

I lay awake the rest of the night. I know our people's history is full of such visits, but I could not believe it could happen to me. I did not tell my mother, Joseph, or any of my friends. I thought they would think I was crazy because I was having the same thoughts.

I missed my first bleeding time, then a second, and I thought, "Could it all be true? I am to be a mother!" How was I to tell Joseph, when I have no idea how it happened? I cried and cried, as I had learned to love Joseph deeply and wanted very much to become his wife.

I finally told my mother the whole story and she looked disbelieving but told me not to worry, everything would be fine. She said she would tell both my father and Joseph when the time was right.

When she told my father, he immediately came and embraced me. He told me how much he loved me and said he and my mother would take good care of me and my baby.

The day my mother summoned Joseph to the house, I waited in my room. I could hear my mother's voice, but not a sound from Joseph. Then I heard the door open and close. I ran out of my room and he was gone. I started to follow him out of the house, but Mother said to give him some time to think it over. It had been a great shock to him. He thought I had been unfaithful and did not believe the story about the angel. I did not blame him.

What was to become of me? I could be stoned to death for his suspicions and, if not that, he had the right to divorce me. How shameful and humiliating for both of us. I was so distressed and confused, and feared I had lost Joseph forever.

But, to my surprise, several days later he came to the house and said the betrothal would continue. I would be his wife. He

17

would love and care for both me and the child for the rest of his life. I could not believe my ears.

"How did this miracle happen?" I asked, and he told us of a visit by the angel Gabriel during the previous night. The angel told him exactly what I was told and said that Joseph was chosen to be the earthly father and protector of me and my child.

I am still in awe of having responsibility for another human being, much less the son of the Almighty. Kathryn, I do not feel special or worthy of such an endeavor. I am a young woman who has had a tremendous responsibility thrust upon her. I do not know if I can meet those responsibilities. I go directly from being my father's beloved daughter to being with child and a wife. There is much to ponder. It is all too much.

I told Joseph I wanted to go to Judah to visit my cousin Elizabeth and share the news with her. Elizabeth has been like a second mother to me and the angel Gabriel told me she is with child after many barren years. It will give me time away from Nazareth, time to be with Elizabeth and for me to adjust to all that has happened. He was so kind and said he would accompany me and, when I was ready, he would return to bring me home to Nazareth.

I hope that Joseph agrees to stop and visit with you on the way to Elizabeth's. I would like to ask him when he comes to visit me, but I have been asking for a lot from him lately.

I hope I am able to have faith and maybe, one day, understand all that has happened. One thing of which I am sure is Joseph. I know the child and I will be safe and greatly loved.

Pray that I may grow in wisdom and faith.

Your good friend's daughter,

Mary

To Kathryn, a faithful follower of the Almighty.

I am Zechariah, Servant of Yahweh and husband of Elizabeth. I am writing to share with you unbelievable news. I have been doing a lot of writing lately, since I cannot speak. I have been mute since an angel announced to me that Elizabeth and I were to have a child, a son.

I was in the Sanctuary in Jerusalem, praying and burning incense when the angel appeared. I was quite frightened. He said our prayers have been answered. I wondered what prayers he was referring to, since Elizabeth is well beyond childbearing age. We had given up all hope of ever having a child of our own and had stopped praying for one.

You know what shame we felt all those years we were childless. We wondered what sin we were guilty of, to be punished in such a cruel way. It was even worse for Elizabeth. She felt disgraced and had long periods of depression until Anne and Joachim's daughter was born.

Mary's birth was a gift to us, as well as to her parents. Elizabeth loved Mary as if she were her very own. She brought joy, love, and peace into our home each time she came to visit. She truly saved Elizabeth's life and I was grateful to Anne and Joachim for sharing their daughter with us. And now, we are to have our very own child, a son!

Since I questioned the angel's message, he struck me dumb until the day the child is named John. Because I cannot speak, I seem to have become a bystander, an observer of my own voiceless life. It has given me much quiet and prayer time—something I was missing with my many responsibilities at the Temple. My prayer time has given me the only relief from my worries. I worry I am too old to be a good father; I worry that if I should become ill or die, there would be no one to care for Elizabeth and the child; I worry Elizabeth may not be able to carry the child to term, or, if she does, something might happen to her or the baby during the birth. I worry that God will punish me for worrying.

Elizabeth, on the other hand, is ecstatic in her pregnancy, and the household with her. Please keep us in your prayers, that all will be well with Elizabeth and the baby. I could not bear to lose my dear wife. She is so precious to me.

Shalom,

Zechariah

To Kathryn, from your spiritual daughter, Mary.

I am not sure how much you know of this, but my mother and her cousin Elizabeth grew up together and were like sisters. They have many, many stories of their youth, the pranks they played on each other, and their betrothals and marriages, which took place about the same time.

Mother told me how very sad she felt for Elizabeth, with each of her own pregnancies, since Elizabeth seemed unable to conceive. Many prayers were said, begging God for a child for Elizabeth and Zechariah, but it was not to be.

When I was born, the third child and first daughter to my family, Elizabeth was there as usual to help my mother. As my mother tells the story, it was love at first sight for Elizabeth. From that day forward, it was as if I had two mothers. There were two women who loved me unconditionally, who nurtured and cared for me, each in her own way. Even when Elizabeth and Zechariah moved, I went to visit them often, always with my mother's blessings. She knew I was Elizabeth's surrogate daughter.

I took all this love and attention for granted. It was just the way it was. I felt nothing would ever change it. When I married and had children, they would have two grandmothers.

Now I am not so sure. I was always the center of Elizabeth's universe. She was always there when I needed her. She shared my joys, my sorrows, my fears, and now she will have her own child. Where does that leave me? How can I share these thoughts and feelings with her, about her pregnancy as well as mine, when her focus now is on her pregnancy, her child?

I know this sounds petty, self-centered, and childish. And I know it is exactly all those things, but how can I change the way I am feeling? Elizabeth is mine and I do not want to share her. This has been a very difficult time for me, and I need her now more than ever.

Joseph and I leave in the morning for Judah to visit her. I feel very conflicted. What if she has no room in her heart for me? What if I am unable to accept the changes in her? What if I continue to resent her baby, her happiness? I just want to be held and nurtured by her. I just want to be a child, and not someone's mother.

My mother tells me not to worry, that all will be well, but how is that to be? She tells me to pray, but my mind is a jumble of thoughts and I cannot even do that. She tells me the heart is capable of holding many loves, never dislodging one for another, always growing and making room.

So, there it is. Do I sound like I am ready to be a mother? I do not think so. I am tired all the time. I cry easily and I feel overwhelmed, thinking of the future. I will let you know how the visit turns out. It is difficult to comprehend it all—Elizabeth and I pregnant at the same time. Please pray for me, since I cannot pray for myself.

Love,

Mary

To my dear Kathryn, from your relieved spiritual daughter, Mary.

I arrived at Elizabeth and Zechariah's home about a week ago. As Joseph and I entered the courtyard, Elizabeth called out to me. She came forward, knelt before me, placed her hands on my belly, and said, "My Lord and my God." She then stood, wrapped her arms around me, and kept repeating, "My beloved daughter," as she stroked my hair and kissed my face.

We both began to cry and sob as I clung to her, telling her how frightened I had been about losing her. I freely shared with her my thoughts and petty jealousies. Joseph and Zechariah stood back, looking distressed and puzzled. I could not stop sobbing. Elizabeth continued to embrace me as she walked me into the house.

I lay on a sleeping mat and she bathed my face with cool scented water, then my hands and feet. She loosened my robes, all the time humming a song she sang to me as a little girl. I fell asleep with Elizabeth sitting next to me, looking at me with such love and devotion it brought more tears to my eyes—tears of happiness.

When I awoke, she was still there. She seemed to know exactly what had happened to me, even before I spoke. She said her child leapt in her womb in the presence of his Lord. She had prepared a great feast for the two of us and we sat together for hours, sharing our unbelievable stories. I don't know where Joseph and Zechariah were, but she made sure those first few hours were just for us.

As you can see, all my fears were groundless. Joseph will be leaving for Nazareth in a few days. I will try to be of some help and comfort to Elizabeth during this time. I owe her so much. God is great!

Your good friend,

Mary

To my dear Kathryn, it's Mary again.

I wanted to let you know how things are going at Elizabeth's. I am feeling much better. I am able to eat without feeling nauseous and I am sleeping very well, so I am not so tired all the time. People even remark about how well I look. They say I have a glow about me. It must be the light of the Spirit, because I feel surrounded and protected by an energy that I am unable to describe.

Elizabeth's time is growing near and she is doing very well. I am learning much from her as I watch her in her roles of wife, friend, confidante, and expectant mother. We prepare together for our babies, sewing infant clothes, blankets, and diapers. We cook special food for the household and Elizabeth's appetite is mighty to behold. We talk about correct feeding techniques, how long a child should stay on the breast. If it has to do with childbearing and rearing, we talk about it.

We massage each other's feet and back, take walks, sing songs, and pray together. Elizabeth has taken the lead in family prayers since Zechariah still cannot speak. He alternates between looking very worried and looking like a young man in the throes of a new love when he is with Elizabeth. The house is full of love and joy—what better place to bear and give birth to a child that is so desperately wanted! I am also anxious for Zechariah to regain his voice. We have much to share about our heavenly visitors.

I occasionally have periods of being frightened and worry for my future. I miss Joseph very much, but he writes long, lovely, and loving letters and that helps. I will return to Nazareth shortly after Elizabeth's baby is born, to be with Joseph and my family for the birth of my child.

You are always in my prayers,

Mary

Dear Kathryn, this is Elizabeth again.

My time grows near. I wish you could see me. My belly sticks out like a huge melon. I have not seen my feet for months, I need help getting into and out of bed and seats, and it often feels like I have to pass water every 30 minutes. The baby must be very strong; it feels like he is stretching his arms and pushing his little feet against the inside of me, so hard that my belly gets very firm. Finally, my appetite has gone back to normal. There was a time when I pitied the person that got between me and the food.

The other night, I woke up to pass water, as usual, and there was Zechariah, lying on his side, one hand propping up his head, the other hand resting gently on my abdomen. He was looking at me with tears in his eyes. He is such a good man.

Yesterday, he brought me a flower from the garden. He began gesturing to me, because a pen was nowhere to be found. He held the bud tenderly, touched my face with it, and raised his arms to heaven in wide, sweeping motions. This went on for several minutes, with him getting frustrated because I could not understand him. Then I said, "Zechariah, are you trying to tell me I am as beautiful as this flower?" He smiled and nodded yes. We both had tears in our eyes as we embraced—not that he can get very close to me at this point in time!

We have had a very long life together, some very difficult and painful times, but, through it all, I was always sure of his love and devotion. It feels as if this pregnancy has intensified the love we have for each other.

Mary has been another blessing during this time. It is the longest she has ever been with us. We are truly a family. What more could a woman ask? I have no fears, no worries about what is to come. I feel a peacefulness beyond belief. My soul rests in the presence of Yahweh.

Shalom to you, my friend,

Elizabeth

To Kathryn, greetings from Zechariah, a very anxious father-to-be.

Elizabeth has been in labor for the last eight hours. The women are inside, attending to her, and I sit out here in the courtyard with my friends. I tried to see her, but they say that it is no place for a man. They look at me as if I am more trouble than I am worth. I am in such agony. Waiting is the worst. I am waiting for news, any news, about how she is doing, how much longer it will be. Every now and then, a woman will come to the door and shake her head, saying, "Nothing yet."

There is almost a party-like atmosphere here in the courtyard—for everyone but me, that is. The men are playing games, drinking wine, eating, and laughing. I can do none of these things, so I thought I would write you and let you know what is happening.

Elizabeth's moans have grown louder. They have the sound of an animal in pain, and mixed in with the groans are some terrible retching noises. It sounds like her insides are being disgorged. The men tell me it will be a long time yet—she has yet to start to scream. I do not think I can stand this. What were we thinking when we prayed so desperately for a child? My only prayer now is for Elizabeth to be free of pain. I would be lost without her. We are as one. She alone knows all there is to know about me and still loves me unconditionally.

The men look at me and smile. I want to scream at them, "What is there to smile at?!" I want to smash their smirking faces. Yahweh, help me! I should be in there beside her, helping her, but what would I do? I feel so helpless. Oh, what am I to do? My aged heart may not be able to tolerate this.

Wait, something has happened.

Kathryn, it's now late at night. Elizabeth's servant Joanna came out to the courtyard and said, "The baby has been delivered, praise God!" I thought to myself, "This cannot be! She has not yet started to scream." Joanna could see my shock and assured me that all was well. I am the father of a healthy son. I sat back down, put my head in my hands, and began to sob.

In a short time, I was allowed into the room. Elizabeth was sitting up against the wall, radiant and smiling, holding a wrinkled red baby. She looked like the previous eight hours had not occurred. She handed me my son and, as I held him in my arms, I began to cry again. This tremendous feeling of love washed over me. I was in awe of this miracle I held. I knew there was nothing I would not do for this child. I would die for him, if need be.

The rabbi who had come in with me asked what the child was to be called, so that he might record the name. Elizabeth said "John." What a stir that caused! People were asking which of our relatives was called John. They said she must be mistaken, the baby should be named for my father. I took the slate and wrote, "The baby is to be called John." With that, I was able to speak. Oh, the mighty power of God!

I am so fatigued. I can barely keep my eyes open. I close this letter as I prepare to go to my bed for the night, there to hold my beloved Elizabeth in my arms and finally tell her how much I love her after so many months of silence.

Thank you for your many prayers.

Zechariah

To Kathryn, greetings from Joseph of Nazareth.

I leave tomorrow for Judah to bring Mary home to Nazareth. Elizabeth has had her baby and is doing fine. Mary sent word to come and get her. It has been a long and lonely time with Mary gone. When Mary told me she wanted to go and visit her cousin, I tried to understand her reasons. I know how much she loves Elizabeth and needed her support, but it was difficult for me not to show my disappointment. I wanted to be the one Mary turned to for love and support, the one she wanted to be with in this important time. But it was not to be. I left Mary with Elizabeth and I am not sure she even realized I was gone.

I returned to Nazareth feeling sad, but knowing Mary would be with me again in a short time. When I received her letter, telling me she had decided to stay there until Elizabeth had her baby, I felt completely rejected and abandoned. I was angry. I was hurt, confused, and embarrassed. How could she treat me this way? I was the new husband who agreed to a platonic relationship because of her fears. Did I not stand by her in the early days of her pregnancy? I did not try to dissuade her when she wanted to visit Elizabeth.

Initially, I wanted to leave the relationship—let her know how it feels to be treated this way. Her letter said it would be months before I would see her again. She wrote, "I know you will understand." She was wrong. I did not understand. I tried to bury my feelings by keeping busy. I took on extra work during the day and, in the evening, did many jobs for my parents as well as Mary's. I spent many hours working on our new home. I collapsed into bed at night and the first thought that would come into my head was what the village must think. Do they also see me as an abandoned husband?

Mary wrote often, but her letters did nothing to alleviate my feelings of despair. The letters were full of news of the household, and of her advancing pregnancy. At the end of the letter, she would casually mention that she missed me. Well, when I could stand it no longer, I wrote to her. I told her of my sufferings, my anger, my fears, and my embarrassment; my feelings of being rejected, unappreciated, and abandoned. I bared my soul.

Kathryn, I cannot tell you how much healing took place in the writing of that letter. A veil lifted and I was able to look at the situation with some objectivity. I recognized my prideful reaction, my fear of my inadequacies, my need to be needed, and my feeling of envy. After thanking God for the blessing of insight I had received, I slept restfully for the first time in months.

In the morning, I did not send the letter. The next week, I received a letter from Mary. It was filled with her feelings of longing and love for me. She shared her fears and emotions, really for the first time. Each letter we wrote thereafter has contained more and more of our hopes, dreams, and love for each other. Our relationship grew and deepened during our separation, through those ensuing letters—another Divine blessing.

So, tomorrow we will be reunited and tonight I cannot sleep with the excitement of the reunion. She left Nazareth a girl and returns a woman, large with child. My prayer is that I may be worthy to be husband and father to this holy pair. Pray for us.

Shalom,

Joseph

Greetings from Joanna, as written by the scribe Micah.

So much has happened since last we spoke. The mistress had her baby and the master has regained his voice. There had been much work to do since the announcement of Elizabeth's pregnancy. Not just the preparation for the baby, but Mary's arrival, Zechariah's muteness, and many, many visitors all contributed to the increased workload. Not one of the servants in the household minded; we have always been treated like part of the family. We all rejoiced and praised God for the miracle of Elizabeth's pregnancy. We tried to make her time easier, but she had so much energy that she worked circles around us almost until the time of her delivery.

The days following the birth were full of excitement and activity. Joseph arrived to accompany Mary home to Nazareth. What a devoted couple they seem, so much in love. She seems like such a child. Joseph, on the other hand, has a quiet maturity that will serve the couple well during Mary's growing-up process.

Before they left, we had a great feast with the entire household in attendance. Mary and Zechariah told of their visits by the angel. They spoke of the similarities and the differences, of their fears and anxieties, and why the master was stricken dumb. Both agreed they had much to learn and, after the initial shock of the visitations, they returned to their usual behavior of obeying the word of God and living out their deep faith in the Almighty. They said this faith allowed them to even more deeply trust and accept their destinies.

Interestingly enough, it was Zechariah, speaking about his loss of speech, that people seemed to listen to most intently. We all could somehow understand and identify with what he was saying. His voice was soft and gentle, kind and strong. It was as if he was speaking with a new voice, one we had never heard before.

He shared deep wisdom with us. He spoke of his frustration, pain, and anger at his inability to share this thoughts and feelings. He wondered out loud if, in the past, he had used or not used his voice in a manner that displeased God. He wondered if he even mattered, without the ability to speak.

He also spoke of the power of the voice, the power to protect ourselves and others, to create moments of love, intimacy, reassurance, and safety. We also have the power to hurt, maim, and even cripple with our words. He spoke of the damage we do to ourselves and our relationships when we choose not to share our pain and hurts. Instead, we bury them deep within our bodies. He said, "My voice has become something to be valued and honored, and I feel blessed to have lost it and blessed to have regained it."

And I feel blessed to be a servant in the house of two such devoted servants of the Lord.

Joanna, as scribed by Micah ben Reuben

To my dear Kathryn, your traveler Mary has returned home, praise God.

Joseph and I returned yesterday from Judah. I am tired from the trip, but otherwise in good health. I was a little worried about how Joseph would react when he saw me *huge* with child, but he looked at me with such love and devotion, I knew there was nothing to be concerned about. All my concerns melted away.

During our trip home, we talked and talked. We caught up on all the local gossip and family news. We shared our thoughts and feelings and just got reacquainted. When we reached Nazareth, we first went to my parents' home. It was so good to see them after so many months. I think my father had some problems seeing me pregnant for the first time. I guess it will take him some time to get used to it.

My mother had prepared a welcoming supper with all my favorite foods. After we ate, she showed me all the clothes she had sewn for the baby. We both had tears in our eyes as we looked at those tiny garments.

Later that day, when I walked into the home Joseph had prepared for us, I was taken aback. His love shone everywhere I looked. He made a beautiful cradle for our baby. It was sitting in the middle of the room with the light from the window shinning upon it. It seemed to have a life of its own as it radiated a warm, soft, welcoming glow. I know it took Joseph many, many hours to create such a masterpiece.

So now, we wait. In a few months, God's masterpiece will be born. It is so good to be home. Please keep in touch and keep us in your prayers.

Love,

Mary

JESUS' BIRTH AND EARLIEST YEARS

To Kathryn, greetings from Joseph of Nazareth.

Mary and I leave tomorrow for Bethlehem. We go to register for the census, as dictated by the Roman authorities. Every day, I pray to God that the Jewish nation may one day be free to rule itself and that the Romans leave our land. For now, we have no choice but to obey or face the consequences.

Mary has several weeks before the baby is to be delivered. We plan to be back in Nazareth in no more than two weeks. The baby will be born here at home, with Mary's family on hand to help with the birth.

I have purchased a small donkey for Mary to ride. It will also carry our supplies. I am worried about her comfort, but she says it will be an adventure. She is bringing her needlework to work on for the few days we will be in Bethlehem. She always makes the best of any difficult situation.

I am very worried, but am trying not to show it. Mary's parents are also worried about the journey, so I am trying to allay their fears, while dealing with my own anxieties. I want to be prepared for any contingency—if, by chance, Mary's time comes, we will find shelter in an inn and stay until Mary is able to travel.

Please keep us in your thoughts and prayers: for Mary and the baby's safety and wellbeing, and that the trip goes smoothly.

Shalom,

Joseph

To my dear Kathryn, from a very joyful new mother Mary!

I have a beautiful, healthy baby boy! His head is covered with black hair, and he has gorgeous, dark brown eyes. He is well-formed and of a good size. His name is Jesus.

I still cannot believe he is mine, and I am a mother. When I looked at him for the first time, I thought my heart would explode. It was difficult to take a breath and I cried tears of happiness. Joseph stood there, looking down at the two of us with such love it made me tremble. What can I say about Joseph? He has been my stalwart protector, guide, provider, and comforter—and yes, even my midwife. Who am I to deserve such a man?

Let me tell you the whole story. We were about a day's journey from Bethlehem. We had just finished our morning meal and were preparing to leave the inn when my labor began. I chose not to mention it to Joseph. I did not want him to worry; the contractions were mild, and I thought we had time to reach Bethlehem and find a midwife and shelter.

The discomfort was slight, and I intermittently walked and rode the donkey. As time went on and the discomfort increased, I was more comfortable walking. We walked hand in hand, talking about the baby, wondering what kind of parents we would be. The prospect of parenthood has been somewhat overwhelming for both of us.

We were in the middle of nowhere when we stopped for the midday meal at a small oasis. The weather was perfect: not too hot, a slight breeze, and scattered clouds, which were a treat since we seldom have a cloudy sky. We had finished eating and were resting in the shade when my water broke.

I was forced to tell Joseph what had just happened. He paled before my very eyes. His eyes glazed over and he did not speak a word. He stood there, not moving, and I started to get nervous.

The pain in the small of my back had become stronger, but not unbearable. He looked terrified and, to tell the truth, my anxiety was increasing.

I called his name several times before he was able to rouse himself. He then began to ask me questions—questions about the pain, the time between contractions, was I hungry, was I thirsty, what position made me most comfortable. He gathered information like a centurion planning a campaign.

He said he thought we had time to reach Bethlehem. He had fed and watered the donkey, and both the animal and I had rested. He told me he had a plan. We would go slowly, so the jostling of the donkey would be kept to a minimum. He felt we should reach Bethlehem well before nightfall. We would go directly to the nearest inn, get me settled, and then find the midwife. He went on to say that he would not leave me alone with a stranger to deliver our baby—he would be with me through the entire birth process. "I promise both you and the baby will be safe and well cared for," he declared.

So, we began the last part of our journey and I was getting more anxious by the hour. What if we did not reach Bethlehem in time? What if we could not find a midwife? I was praying to Yahweh, "Give me the courage to endure what must be," but my faith was wavering. I always believed Yahweh would love, protect, and provide if I obeyed the customs and rules of Judaism, but now I was not sure of that. Did Yahweh really care about my labor pains?

By the time we reached the outskirts of Bethlehem in midafternoon, the pains had become closer together and more intense, but still remained in the small of my back. The women at home had told me labor could start that way, but would eventually move around to my belly as the time neared for the birth. So, I thought I still had plenty of time.

We stopped at the first inn we came to, for which I was grateful, and Joseph asked for a room. The man laughed as he told us he had no rooms. "Where do you expect to find a room this late in the day, with so many people in town for the census?" he asked. Joseph assured me he would find a place, no matter what the cost. But cost was not the issue. We went to several more places, all with same results: "Sorry, no room."

We reached the southern outskirts of town and came to another inn. I could not help but cry out in pain. Joseph was frantic to find lodging. He told the owner of our plight and said that I could go no further. The man said there were no rooms and that people were even sleeping on the floor of the dining area. Joseph said he would pay any price, do any work, if only we could stay.

The man heard my cries and Joseph's pleading and said we could use the cave behind the inn, where he sheltered his animals. His name was Samuel and he was very kind and generous. He said he had just brought in fresh hay and it was warm and protected from the weather.

He offered to bring us some food, fresh water, lanterns, and blankets. We thanked him for everything and accepted everything except the food, for by that time I was nauseous and retching. (Food was the last thing I wanted to see or smell, and Joseph was okay with that.)

Joseph got us into the cave, made a fire at the entrance, prepared for the birth, spoke to and patted down the animals, then said he was going to find a midwife. I screamed for him not to leave me, because I didn't think it would be much longer.

He did not leave. He stayed by my side, praying aloud, asking Yahweh for help, over and over. This went on for what seemed like an eternity. My body felt as if someone was breaking my back. During that time, he rubbed my feet, massaged my back, and told me stories of his childhood and what a mischievous boy he had been. He made me smile between the contractions. The nausea and retching increased with each contraction. He wiped my face with a cool cloth and told me, over and over, how much he loved me. He told me to breathe, "Breathe, Mary, breathe." Do not ask me how, but Joseph knew exactly what to do.

At some point, it became one long, torturous, back-breaking pain. I was drenched in sweat. Eventually, the baby began to emerge. "Push, Mary, push!" Joseph urged me. "Our beloved son is about to be born!" Finally, with one last great effort and scream, the baby was delivered and he let out a lusty cry.

Joseph gently held the baby, gazing at him with such amazement and awe. He pulled some string from his belt, wrapped it around the cord, then cut it, wrapping the baby in a blanket and placing him in my arms. Then he massaged my belly until the afterbirth was delivered. He placed it in a pail Samuel had brought for wastes.

I put the baby to my breast and he began to suckle. What a sensation! I could feel my womb begin to contract. Joseph sat there, watching us. Soon the baby dozed off and Joseph brought me water to drink—I was so parched!—and a dry blanket. He lay next to me, with his arms wrapped gently around me. We fell asleep. We were so exhausted. What a sleep that was: a sleep full of sweet dreams. I wasn't sure what was real or what was a dream, me holding my miracle baby in my arms and Joseph holding me in his.

I am not sure how long we slept, but we woke when we heard the animals stirring. We lay there, feeling completely rested, rejuvenated, and famished. Joseph rose and fed and watered the animals. After the animals were tended to, he took the baby, placed him in a nearby manger, gave me water to drink, and helped me bathe with water from the animal's trough and put on fresh clothes. Since I was still bleeding, he fashioned a diaper for me out of some of the materials I had brought. I lay there on the fresh-smelling hay, clean and warm, with the two people I loved most in the whole world, and marveled at how this had come to be.

Joseph had finished his bathing and had stepped out to empty the waste bucket when all of the animals—two cows, one goat, and our donkey—began to move around. The cows walked over to the manger, looking for food, I supposed. I started to get up, concerned for the baby, when both cows stopped, leaned over the manger, lowed softly, and breathed on Jesus. It became very still.

Kathryn, in the dark of the night, I could see some kind of light pass between the animals and the baby. The whole cave brightened and there was a tangible energy in the air. It was as bright as day inside the cave. The cows stayed there for several minutes before they returned to their stalls, as if to make room for the other animals. Next, the donkey came forward, followed by the goat. Each repeated the breathing on the baby, transmitting some kind of energy.

Joseph returned just as they had moved away from the manger. I thought about telling him what had happened, but he said, "I am hungry. I am going to the inn to get some food." I decided it could wait, because I was hungry too.

Joseph returned with a great feast that Samuel had been preparing for us: sweet apricot nectar, still-warm bread, goat cheese, dates, figs, and oh! such delicious, sweet halvah. Never had food tasted so good. Joseph said Samuel would be down soon. He wanted to see the baby.

I began to tell Joseph about the animals and he listened in wonder. We talked, ate, and marveled every time we looked at Jesus. I might add—what a good baby he is! He fusses only if he is hungry or wet. There was such peace, such joy, such contentment in that little cave; even the animals had become part of our family and the miracle of this birth.

Soon Samuel called from the outside of the cave and asked permission to enter. He brought with him some of his dead wife's belongings, things he thought I might use: a shawl, some underclothing, a mantle, a dress, and even the cloths she used during her monthly bleeding time. She must have died very young, and he said they had no children.

He approached the manger to see the baby and, instead of leaning over, he knelt next to it to look in. He knelt that way for several minutes, without saying a word, all the while gently caressing Jesus' cheek with his hand. Finally he stood, turned to look at us with tears in his eyes, and, with deep emotion in his voice, thanked us for this great honor. Then he turned and walked back to the inn.

The night was full of mysterious happenings. About an hour or so later, several men approached the cave. They stood at the entrance, not saying anything, just looking in. Finally, Joseph asked, "What is it you seek?"

The eldest of the four replied, "My name is Eli. This is Nathan, David, and Joshua. We are shepherds. We were tending our flocks when a light appeared in the sky. It was so bright, as when the sun shines at midday."

Then, one of the other shepherds interrupted, "Yes, and there was music, beautiful music! Voices, singing, 'Glory to God in the highest, and on earth, peace to men of good will.' It was music like I never heard before. We dropped to the ground in fear and covered our faces. I thought it was the end of the world."

"Nathan," Eli said impatiently, "I thought we agreed I would be the one to speak." Then Eli continued the story.

"We heard a voice say, 'Do not be afraid!' We looked up and saw an angel. The angel continued, 'For today in the city of David a savior has been born to you, who is the Messiah and Lord. This will be a sign for you: You will find him wrapped in swaddling clothes and lying in a manger.' Then, suddenly, it became dark again. I looked over at Nathan, to see if he had seen and heard the things I had. He looked dumbstruck and just stared at me.

"Then we heard running footsteps in the dark. Joshua and

David, who were on the other side of the hill, tending their flocks, called out, 'Did you see it, and did you hear it?' The four of us sat around the fire, talking about what we had seen and heard and what we should do. Were we all crazy? Why would a newborn child be in a manger? Who has a baby in a stable? Should we go and find this place? Who would tend the flocks? What would we say when we get there? Do we all go or do some stay with the sheep?

"We finally decided all of us would go and see if it were true. And here is the baby, just as the angel said. Praise to Yahweh, the Jewish nation will be saved! The Romans will be vanquished! We will be free men in the land of Israel."

Kathryn, it took my breath away. They seemed to think my baby is to become the King of Israel. I invited them to come in and see the baby, saying, "His name is Jesus." All four men knelt before the manger and seemed to pay homage to him. After a short time, Nathan turned to me to ask if he could hold him. I nodded yes.

As all the men stood, Joseph reached into the manger and gently lifted out his son. He laid the swaddled Jesus in Nathan's arms. Nathan held Jesus with such tenderness and murmured sweet words to him. He then turned to me and, with tears in his eyes, asked if the others could hold him. They passed Jesus from one to another, as if a great and holy gift was being offered.

Joshua was the last to hold him. Then he brought him to me. Tears also shone in his eyes as he thanked me for such a great honor. It was the second time we heard those words about honor that night. They sat with us for a short time longer, telling us about themselves, and then said they had to get back to their flocks.

After they left, I thought, "I will have much to tell my son of the night that he was born." Joseph and I talked for several hours about the birth and the mysterious occurrences of the night. Would we ever understand it all? How could the birth

43

of one child evoke such responses from humans and animals alike? We talked about our families and how elated they will be to have a grandson. Their love for him will have no bounds. I cannot wait to share my child with them.

We will probably leave for Nazareth in about five days. I will be well rested and recovered by that time. My heart beats in anticipation of returning home to all those who love me and mine.

From Mary, with much joy!

To Kathryn, greetings from Joseph of Nazareth, husband of Mary and father of Jesus.

As you read this letter, Mary, Jesus, and I are on our way to Egypt. Yes, Egypt! I know—one more thing that is hard to believe. We have left Bethlehem, not to return to our home in Nazareth, but to flee to Egypt.

Mary shared her letter to you with me, telling of the birth of Jesus, so I will begin my explanation with the second day following the baby's birth. Samuel, the innkeeper, returned to the cave in the late morning to tell us there was now room in the inn. We could move in anytime we were ready.

Believe it or not, we had mixed emotions about a move. The cave had become such a special, holy place for us, a place of miracles, love, and joy. We did not even want to leave the animals—but, of course, we did; common sense prevailed. We said goodbye to the animals, then I helped Mary and the baby. We moved our belongings to the inn.

The room Samuel gave us must be, by far, the largest in the inn; it is so spacious, clean, and comfortable. I knew we would be content there until Mary regained her strength and we could return to Nazareth. So, we settled in, and I registered with the census.

We had been there about a week, Mary was getting stronger, and we began preparations for the journey home. We both were very enthusiastic about returning to Nazareth. Mary was beside herself with excitement. She packed and repacked two days before we were planning to leave. She was unable to sit for a minute, jumping up to check on something one more time.

She asked me, more than once, "What do you think my mother will say when she sees the baby? What do you think your mother will say?" Then, not waiting for an answer, she went on to talk about how they will love him intensely, recognize what a special baby he is, and how beautiful and good he is.

After dinner that night, Samuel come to the room, very flustered, and said, "There are three royal personages asking to see the child."

I thought at first that he might be making a joke, but he assured me he was serious. He went downstairs to escort them to our room. Mary and I looked at each other and said, practically at the same time, "Now what?" Mary was sitting on our bedding and leaning against one wall, holding Jesus in her arms. I stood by her side as they entered the room.

They came in quietly, not saying a word, and knelt before Mary and the baby. Each one placed a small traveler's chest at her feet. They were dressed in royal garb, and moved and held themselves in a way rulers do—except for the kneeling. We were dumbstruck.

They rose to their feet and began telling their story. They were astrologers from the east, each from a different kingdom. But each had the same dream, night after night, telling them the greatest and most holy king was about to be born. A star in the heavens would lead them to this king. They were directed to contact each other and begin the journey in search of this babe. The star would guide them.

It had taken them weeks to find us. What determination and faith they had in their mission! They did not know where they were going: resting by day, following the star at night, asking along the way if any had heard of the birth of this new king.

When they arrived in Judah, they went to King Herod and asked if he knew of the birth. The King met with his priests, who confirmed there was such a prophecy: A king shall be born in Bethlehem. He then asked that they go find this child and return to him with the news so he could also pay homage.

The star brought them to the inn. It was still overhead as they told their story. The night before their visit, they had another dream, in which they were told not to return to Herod, but to leave for the east by a different route. The angel in the dream said we were in danger.

Samuel brought refreshments and we shared our experiences since we had arrived in Bethlehem. We opened their gifts and they explained the spiritual significance of gold, frankincense, and myrrh. Then they left. Once again, Mary and I had much to ponder. We wondered what lay in store for our son. We went to bed early, thinking we might leave in the morning, depending on the weather and how Mary was feeling.

I had been asleep only a short time when I awoke from a dream. An angel had come to me in the dream and said, "The child is in danger. You must flee to Egypt immediately." When I told Mary, she was very upset. She cried and pleaded, "Let us just go home to Nazareth!" I have never seen her so distraught. The thought of not going home was unbearable for her.

After she quieted, I explained that all the messages delivered thus far had come true, and we had best obey this one. So, we finished packing, woke Samuel to say goodbye, and left in the middle of the night.

It's been three days since we left Bethlehem. I am giving this letter to a merchant who is heading to your village. He says he will deliver it directly to you.

Please pray for Mary. She is heartbroken, cries frequently, is eating very little and barely speaking. She never fails to meet the baby's needs, so he is thriving, but it seems to take every bit of her energy. We have many days of travel ahead of us and I will write again when we are settled.

Shalom,

Joseph

To Kathryn, from Samuel, Bethlehem innkeeper.

You do not know me, but your friends Mary and Joseph stayed at my inn a short time ago. We became good friends in the short time they were here. They told me I could write to you, to give and receive news concerning them.

We have had a terrible tragedy here in Bethlehem. The word does not fully describe what occurred. I am not sure it was related to the fact that Mary, Joseph, and the baby had been here, but I have a feeling it was. I will try to describe what happened and you can decide for yourself.

Mary, Joseph, and the baby had only been gone one day when we woke in the morning to find the town surrounded by Roman soldiers. They had arrived during the night, made camp, and completely encircled the town. We had no idea what was happening. The townspeople, as well as my guests, were very frightened. Everyone was speculating about the reason for the soldiers being here.

We were just clearing up from the morning meal when soldiers came marching into town. They began to gather all the men and adolescent boys, taking us all to the center of town. The women were ordered to stay in their houses or the inns. They were in a frenzy, standing at the doorways, calling out for their sons and husbands.

After every man and boy had been moved to the front of the town square, the centurion in charge announced that we had nothing to fear, we would not be harmed, this was all part of a military exercise. They then shackled our hands and feet, connecting us one to another. We were now one impotent entity.

Several soldiers were left to guard us and the other soldiers began systematically going from house to house, and also to each inn. We began to hear screams as we never heard before, children crying, soldiers shouting, armor rattling. We tried to move as a group, but it was impossible. We were frantic. Men began yelling out for their families and pleading with the guards to release them.

My sister Judith told me what happened when two soldiers entered her home. She was there with her three children: her eldest, Barabbas; her daughter, Sarah; and her baby, Benjamin. A soldier took the baby from Judith and peeked in the baby's diaper to see if it was boy or girl, then, right before their eyes, he ran the baby through with his sword. It happened so fast, so unexpectedly, that for a few seconds they were unable to move or say a word. My sister ran to her baby, screaming his name, trying to stop the bleeding, but it was of no use. He was dead. Sarah was whimpering, holding onto her mother's skirt. Barabbas just stood, still as a statue, his face a mask of hate as he watched the soldiers leave the house.

This happened in house after house: baby boys murdered— run through with swords, heads smashed against walls, throats slit, tiny necks twisted between soldiers' hands. We knew something horrific was going on. We could smell the fear and even began to smell the blood, but we were helpless.

When every baby boy under the age of two was dead, the soldiers withdrew, broke camp, and retreated. The guards released one of us, then left to rejoin the troops at a fast gallop. It took quite awhile for all of us to get free. As one would be unshackled, he would help the man next to him. We had no chance of catching up with the Romans on foot.

Men rushed to their homes, where women were still screaming, children crying. The men looked at this indescribable carnage and began cursing the Romans. Some even cursed God. It was the only time in my life I was thankful for being childless. A total of 27 baby boys were killed. Not one boy under the age of two survived. Two women were killed and several injured, trying to protect their children.

Two weeks have passed. The burials have taken place and

the cleansing of the town is completed, but the heart of the town is torn apart. Bethlehem will never be the same. We men feel a collective guilt for not protecting the infants and their mothers. The women are moving as if in a trance, and the children no longer smile, play, or laugh. Their eyes are filled with terror. My nephew Barabbas has appeared to turn to stone. He never shed a tear, recoils from his parents' touch, and seems to be in his own private hell. We are very worried about him.

Will we ever recover? I do not think so. I look for some meaning in all of this, but find none. If only we had not believed the centurion, if only we had fought the soldiers! We are filled with "if only"s. Why did this happen? To me, it seems connected to the birth of Jesus. So many miraculous things happened during that time. I just knew a great and holy event had taken place. I think what happened here was the danger the angel warned Joseph about. If only I had realized that, I could have warned the town and maybe saved the lives of those babies. If only, if only—we will go to our graves with those two words on our lips.

I do not know what is going to happen here. We have a collective hate for the Romans, as well as all that guilt. Is this any way to live? Some are talking about moving, others about joining the zealots, and others are not talking at all.

Please let Joseph know what happened here, when you hear from him. He can decide whether to tell Mary or not, but let him know he did the right thing in leaving here.

Pray for Bethlehem.

Samuel

To Kathryn, from Ruth, a survivor of the Bethlehem massacre.

It has been three months since the atrocity took place here in Bethlehem. It was a cool, clear winter morning when the mighty Roman army murdered every boy child under the age of two in our village—a day that is embedded in our memories for all of time.

The town suffered a blow from which it may never recover. It was once a quiet, peaceful, safe place to live, to raise a family, to worship, to be part of a community that supported and cared about all of its inhabitants. That has all changed. No one will ever feel safe again. There are feelings of anger, hatred, and revenge everywhere, and where those feelings are absent, there is a death of the spirit. People go through the motions of life, in a stupor, neither crying nor smiling.

While no child of mine was killed, there was not a child or family who had a loss that I did not know. I am suffering from a pain in my heart and soul that I have never experienced before. I am unable to sleep. I am always on the verge of tears, but unable to cry. I have a pressure in my chest that makes it difficult to take a deep breath. I lack physical energy to do the things necessary to survive. I do not wish to see or talk to anyone.

And, worst of all, is that I am unable to pray. I do not curse God, as some have, but I have lost my connection to Yahweh. I lie in my bed, wishing not to be alive. I berate myself for feeling this way; others have suffered oh, so much more than I, and yet I continue to have these feelings. I am unable to let them go. That sense of helplessness we all felt that horrible day continues.

What could we have done to protect those innocent babes? What can I do now to ensure that it never happens again? What can I do to help our village? What can I do to help myself? I do not know.

A healer from a neighboring town came and said not only are the village and its people suffering grievously, but the blood-soaked earth is wailing at its core for those sweet souls.

The word of this tragedy has spread through all of Israel. People are calling for rebellion against the Romans, even more than usual. More bloodshed—is that the answer?

Samuel, the innkeeper, spoke to me in confidence. He said he thinks this may have occurred because of the birth of a "special child." This child was born on his property about a week before the murders took place. He is unwilling or unable to tell me any more than just that.

He did tell me the cave, and a room in his inn where these people stayed, has some kind of healing energy. He offered to let me stay at the inn. Samuel is a very kind and loving man who has also suffered much. He seems to feel even more guilt then the rest of us.

Kathryn, I go to the inn to spend a few days and will write to you after my stay. I ask, no, I beg for your prayers. I do not know how much longer I can survive.

Ruth

To Kathryn, from a Ruth at peace.

It has been about two weeks since I returned home from Samuel's inn. He was so kind and considerate to me while I was there. He showed me a side of himself that I had never seen before and we have become very good friends.

I am not sure where to begin. I feel changed—not free from the pain or the reality of what occurred, or how the town continues to suffer from its losses, but I am sleeping better. I do not wake up, seeing those horrific scenes in my mind's eye, and I have been able to resume some of my normal activities, due to an increase in my physical energy. The trauma resurrected the wounds of my husband's and my parents' deaths, which I had chosen to bury rather than experience the pain. Being at the inn allowed me to face the past and present wounds. It allowed healing to begin to take a place at its deepest level.

The time spent at the inn was good. There was a tangible energy in both the room and the stable. I spent most of my time in these areas, praying and meditating. There were no great insights. No voices came to me, no dreams or visions, just a quiet presence that caused me to feel that all will be well. I am still struggling with my inner demons, so the journey is to give up the struggle and let Yahweh heal me from the inside out. I am helpless in this. My goal is not to feel hopeless.

The town is making its way toward a superficial normalcy—much the same situation as mine. Healing must come from within the town as well. Just washing away the blood, removing the signs of the killings, will not restore us to health and well-being. I pray that we will all be open to the Divine healing that is available to all. I know in my heart it will be done, in God's time, not mine.

Please continue to pray for me and the town of Bethlehem.

In gratefulness,

Ruth

To Kathryn of Jericho, from Cassius, a centurion in the Roman army.

Your reputation as a holy woman is known throughout all of Israel and I am seeking your help. I was with the troops that entered Bethlehem and killed all those babies. Since that time, I have been suffering from severe headaches that distort my vision and cause me to vomit for hours at a time. Plus, in the past month I have developed boils on the inside of my hands.

I know this is all related to that day. Let me tell you what happened. We received our marching orders and were told that Bethlehem was harboring zealots who had recently attacked and killed several soldiers. We were to exact retribution for this action, teaching them a lesson so they would no longer think it wise to support the rebels. We were told further orders would be given when we reached the town. We arrived late in the night, surrounded the town, and set the guard, seemingly undetected. We even hoped to capture some of the zealots as we entered the town in the morning.

Early the next day, the commander called the centurions together for our final orders. He then told us what the retribution would be: We were to "kill every baby boy under the age of two." There was a great outcry of protest from the men. "We are Roman soldiers, not baby killers!" we said. The commander let the protests go on for a short time, saying nothing, then looking every man directly in the eye said, "These are your orders. If any soldier in your command does not obey, the centurion in charge, as well as the disobedient man, will be killed." After that, we stood as silent as death itself.

The plan was to remove the men from their homes and incapacitate them by shackling them together. Then we would move from house to house in teams of three until the orders were carried out. The soldiers were as resistant to the order as we were, but after being threatened with death, they became still and obedient.

In all my years in the army, I have encountered no more horrific an experience. I was holding one mother back while one of the men checked to see the sex of the baby. She was very still, just watching, not knowing what was happening. Suddenly, she must have realized the danger to her child and became a mother tiger, protecting her cub. She bit and scratched. She had great strength as she tried to get free of my grasp. She squirmed, she wiggled, she spit in my face, screaming for her husband to help. In the struggle, we both fell to the floor and I lay atop her to keep her still. Finally she became quiet. The baby had been killed, of course. When I stood, I saw the mother too was dead; my weight had crushed the breath from her body.

This scene was taking place all over the village. We could hear the women wailing, the men yelling and cursing, the other children crying and calling out for their mothers. It was complete chaos. We had a hard time controlling the cohort. Some were attempting to rape the women and loot the village. An evil force had been unleashed in even the most disciplined of the soldiers.

We were there a very short time, but we made enemies for many generations to come. When we were finished, we all moved in silence, some of us covered with blood, unable to look at one another. We made our way back to camp to pick up our gear and leave the area as quickly as possible.

The silence continued as we rode back to Jerusalem. "How will we be able to live with what we have just done?" I thought. And, as it has come to pass, I have not been able to. I dream about that day, I wake up thinking about it, I see those babies being slaughtered in my head, over and over again.

I do not deserve to live. It would have been better if I had refused the order and been put to death then, rather than to live like this. It does not even matter that I feel this deep remorse;

it will not bring those babies back. There is nowhere to seek forgiveness, nor do I deserve it.

I was writing to you for help, but in the writing the answer has come to me. I will take my life as retribution for my acts. In fact, I have no choice. I cannot live like this. I used to be a man of honor, but no more—that is gone. The pain I feel is unendurable.

I thank you for listening. At least one person will know the deep sorrow one Roman soldier has experienced over this crime against mankind.

Respectfully,

Cassius

To Kathryn from Joseph, late of Bethlehem, now of Egypt.

We have reached Egypt safely. It took us almost three weeks to arrive here. We moved slowly, due to Mary's condition. Every third day or so we stopped and rested for an entire day. There were travelers and merchants along the way who were kind and generous to us. We encountered not one hostile act or attitude. Yahweh truly provides and protects. We reached Egypt about two weeks ago. We found a small Jewish community in a town called Pelusium. The people here have been welcoming and supportive.

Mary's condition is the same now as it was during the trip. She still eats very little, and cries easily and often. She seldom speaks and, when she does, complains of an overwhelming fatigue and apologizes over and over for being such a burden to me. "I am a bad wife and mother," she says. She seldom sleeps, even when Jesus is sleeping. It seems to me she has lost the essence which made her Mary. She is like a different woman. It breaks my heart to see her like this.

I feel so helpless. Day and night, I pray and beg Yahweh for help. I do not know what to do or where to turn. Our mothers would know what to do. I feel so alone and lonely. I want my beloved Mary back. Why is she doing this to me? Why has she abandoned me?

I have not looked for work because I need to be here to care for Jesus and Mary. Mary feeds and bathes the baby, but only with much encouragement. I have been going to market, doing the cooking and cleaning, and even the laundry. I bring Jesus with me whenever I go out and he is fast becoming the darling of this small community. He seems to be thriving through all this.

Mary is not thriving. She has lost weight, is pale, and has dark circles under her eyes. She has to be reminded and helped

57

to bathe and change her clothes. The other night, she cried and cried in my arms, asking, "What is the matter with me?" I try to comfort and reassure her, but it is of little use. I do not have the words or the knowledge to be of help. I have no one to turn to for advice or support. What is to become of us?

[Several days later.]

After rereading this letter, I was not sure I would send it, but something has changed since I wrote those words. I feel optimistic for the first time since this all began. The day after Mary cried in my arms, I was in the marketplace and a neighbor shyly came up to me. She said she did not wish to intrude, but there is a holy man, a healer, whose name is Hiram. She said he lives in the village, and maybe he could help my family.

The next day, I took Jesus and went to see this man. He had heard about our small family and was waiting to hear from me. I explained, as best I could, through my tears, what had happened and our circumstances. What a relief it was to be able to tell someone my troubles! After listening to me, and comforting and supporting me, he went to talk with Mary. He asked Jesus and I to stay in his home. His wife fixed us a meal—it was good to not have to eat my own cooking. I felt relaxed for the first time in weeks. It was as if Hiram and his wife had physically lifted a weight from my heart.

Hiram returned after about two hours and spoke of what had taken place with Mary. Surprisingly enough, Mary spoke at length to him. He did not share what she had said, only that she spoke. When I heard this, I felt irritated and jealous. I did not know why I felt this way, but it felt like—once again—she had shut me out.

Hiram told me that Mary had a spiritual, energetic wound. She had a deep and intense connection with her family and her home. Not being able to go home at such a very vulnerable time—the birth of her first child—it was as if she was ripped from the place where her heart and soul abided. This tearing away opened a wound through which her life force was oozing, draining the energy she needed to function. He performed a healing ceremony with her and promised to return daily until she improved.

When I returned, I found Mary asleep. Her face appeared relaxed for the first time in a long time. I put Jesus down for a nap and finally feel ready to complete this letter.

Please add your prayers to mine for a quick and complete recovery for our beloved Mary.

Joseph

To my friend for life, Kathryn, from Mary.

This letter is an important part of my healing process. Since I cannot be with you at this time of my life, I am writing to you, my parents, and Elizabeth, the people I love most dearly. Joseph told me he wrote and told you of our safe arrival, where we were staying, and of my illness. Indeed, it was an illness, an illness of my spirit, my soul.

I have a great need to share with you what happened to me and what is presently occurring in my life. That night in Bethlehem, when Joseph told me of the angel's visit, telling him that we could not go home to Nazareth, that we must flee to Egypt to protect the baby, I felt the breath rush out of my body. It was as if my chest was wrapped in a tight girdle and it could no longer expand to take in air. I did not take another long, relaxed breath again until just a few weeks ago.

I was heartbroken. I was angry. I was filled with terror. I wanted my mother. I needed my mother. My first child had just been born and I would not be able to share this great joy and tremendous responsibility with my family. How was I to do this without the women in my life?

I was in such emotional pain! It became more intense, the further we got from Nazareth. I could not sleep. I had to force myself to eat and care for the baby. It seemed I was either crying or on the verge of tears. Poor Joseph, he was beside himself. He did not know what to do. I did not know what I wanted him to do. All I did know was I wanted to go home.

I do not remember much of the journey. I felt I was in a state of unreality, that this could not be happening to me. By the time we reached Pelusium, I had lost the energy to be angry and fell into a deep state of despair. There was no light in my life. Everything was dark and filled with threatening shadows. I refused to leave the house. I only spoke if I was spoken to. I fed and cared for Jesus only when Joseph would bring him to me. Joseph helped me bathe, dress, and eat, activities I had to be forced into, for I did not want to do anything. These activities meant life and light and I could not tolerate either.

At night, when Joseph and Jesus were asleep, I would watch them and think they deserved more than this: a good, caring, loving wife and mother. I felt they would be better off without me. My heart and soul were in such torment. I tried to pray, but could not. Where was Yahweh? I berated, blamed, and accused myself of many sins. I was so guilt-ridden and could do nothing to change.

Joseph and Jesus became secondary to this pulsating, all-consuming mass of pain that dwelt in and surrounded me. I did not know who I was anymore. What was to become of me and how much longer could I endure? Never in my life had I felt so selfish, so self-absorbed, and yet so abusive and neglectful of myself. It was as if Mary no longer existed.

Then a miracle happened. Joseph's prayers were answered. A holy man and healer came to me one afternoon, explained who he was, and said that Joseph had asked him for help. He asked me what had happened to me and for some reason I was able to pour out my heart to him. He then had me lie on our sleeping mat. He prayed aloud for me and moved his hands around my body—not touching me. His hand would sometimes hover over my heart or my head. I fell into a deep, relaxed sleep. When I woke, Joseph and Jesus had returned home. Joseph said I had slept for three hours.

Hiram, the healer, came every day for three weeks, listening to me, asking me about my dreams, repeating the same prayers and healing ritual. Each time, I would fall into a deep, untroubled sleep. It is hard to explain how I felt during these ministrations. I felt movement, in and around me—movement I could not see or touch. With my eyes closed, I would see bright, vibrant colors. Several times, I saw my mother's face, which brought tears of happiness to my eyes. Twice a week Deborah, Hiram's wife, would come and massage my body with warm, fragrant oils. I felt nurtured and safe. I started to sleep at night after about a week or so and shortly after that my appetite returned.

Hiram and Deborah sat with Joseph and me on several occasions to listen to our worries and concerns. Hiram explained at some length what has happened to me. I will give you the shortened version. He said that every child is born with intangible and invisible energetic cords connecting them to their parents. As the child grows, these cords grow stronger and more intense, more life-sustaining, especially with the mother. The cords are there, along with the physical presence of the parents, to nurture, nourish, heal, and keep the child well and safe.

As the child grows and matures, these cords begin to weaken, but never completely disappear. It is a gentle evolution of separation and growth. This happens so the blossoming child can become an independent, functioning adult, capable of developing relationships and have children of their own, and so the cycle continues.

But, if this separation occurs before either the child or the parent is ready, or if it is a violent separation, it creates a gaping wound to the soul, just as if a knife had ripped open the heart cavity. It will manifest in emotional and physical symptoms. The wound needs to be tended to and healed, just as you would treat any other injury.

It takes time. Hiram and Deborah still visit me once a week and I feel more myself every day. Hiram suggested I begin writing to my loved ones as part of my healing process. It will keep me connected to all of you during our stay in Egypt.

I know there is more work to do, but in my heart I trust that I will be totally healed. In fact, I am healing and will be a better woman for living through this illness. I feel more compassion, more love, and a deeper understanding of suffering. I know, whatever befalls me in the future, I am better prepared because of this experience. I am able to pray again and feel the presence of Yahweh in my life. I thank the Divine for my life, Joseph, Jesus, and all of my friends and family.

I have met the women in this village and have made two special friends. Jesus is everyone's darling. Not a day goes by without several children stopping by to see him. They take him for rides in a little cart Joseph made for him or they just sit on the floor, watching as he lies on his blanket. The other day, he rolled over for the first time and delighted the children, so they began to clap. Jesus held his little head up and smiled his beautiful smile.

Never again will I take for granted these delights and desires for life, be they large or small. To lie with Joseph, to hold my baby, to watch the sunset, to eat a good meal, to enjoy friends— too many gifts to name, so many things for which to be grateful.

I do not know how long we will be here, but I know the day will come when I will be with my loved ones again.

Thank you for your prayers. I love you dearly,

Mary

Dear Kathryn, from Mary, the mother of two sons.

Good news to share: I recently gave birth to another beautiful baby boy! We named him Joseph, after his father. He is such a good baby and is already sleeping the night through. He had no problem with nursing—he latched on right from the beginning. He is gaining weight and responds to anyone who talks to him. He is almost one month old and has brought much joy to our family. Jesus is such a loving and kind big brother, it is hard to believe he is 3 years old already. He loves to watch Joseph try and roll over and wants to help if he does not make it.

What a difference in their births! You remember how it was with the birth of Jesus in the stable. Well, I had this baby in our home, with a midwife and Joseph, who said, "I delivered my first son. I will not be put outside for the birth of my second child." And he was as supportive as ever, making my labor as easy as labor can be. The labor did not take as long as with the first child, which I am told is not unusual, and I was grateful.

They brought Jesus to me as soon as I delivered the baby. He was so excited. We had been preparing him, but he is still too young to really know what all of it meant. He looked very surprised when he saw the baby for the first time, poked him with his finger, then he crawled over and lay on my other side. I had a son on each arm, Joseph was sitting next to me, and I began to cry with happiness. I think it scared Jesus a little, so he began to pat my cheek, telling me it will be ok. It was more than ok, it was wonderful! I felt ecstatic. What more can a woman ask for: another healthy baby, a husband whom I cherish, and a toddler who brings delight to anyone who meets him?

Joseph and I miss our families, but we have talked often about how we came to be in this village and we both agree we would not have missed this experience because of all the blessings we have received. We have found community, support, and love. We have friends who are like family. Joseph has become the village carpenter. He even has a young boy as an apprentice, Mordechai, whom he loves. He enjoys his work and has many friends.

As for me, I came as a child myself and have become an adult in the past few years. After my post-birth illness, that sickness of the spirit, I have learned much. I now have the skills to help others that may experience similar episodes. I have friends who have taught me how to be a competent mother and wife, sharing their wisdom and even their recipes.

And the biggest thing I have learned is that Yahweh's plans are so much better than mine. There is no way I would have chosen this path, had I been given a choice. In fact, all I wanted to do was go home and be with my family, but I am a better person for this experience. I have a deeper faith and trust in Yahweh because of it.

I know, at some point in time—Yahweh's time, not mine—we will go home and I will be glad to be with family again. But, for now, I will enjoy, love, and support the family we have made here in Pelusium.

It will also be good to see you again. May you be, and remain, in good health.

Love,

Mary

Dear Kathryn, from Mary, your devoted friend and follower.

Good news! Joseph had a dream last night. The angel said it is safe to return to Israel. Praise God! It has been so long since we set foot in our homeland or laid eyes on family and friends.

Joseph and I talked about when we should leave. He really left it up to me, since I am still very fatigued after baby Joseph's birth and he is still waking up during the night for a feeding. It will also take us awhile to prepare for the trip home. We have to sell our belongings and, hardest of all, we must say goodbye to the many friends who have become our family here in Pelusium. We decided to wait until I am feeling up to taking the trip.

I cannot begin to tell you how kind, generous, and welcoming the people in this village have been to us. They have supported us during the early, bad times and rejoiced with us during the many good times. I have learned much from them, especially from Deborah and Hiram. They took me under their wing and taught me much about healing. I was able to help them minister to the people of the village. It was a great blessing for me. Another great blessing was being able to write you, Kathryn, and receive your letters filled with love and wisdom. It made the separation more tolerable, less lonely.

I let my parents know that we would be coming home soon and to find us a place to stay. Hopefully the place Joseph and I called home during the first few months of our marriage is still available. We were very happy there—it seems so long ago.

On our way to Nazareth, we hope to stop in Jericho. I know you read my letters over these past years, filled with news of Joseph and the children. Now, at last, you will be able to see the children for yourself. I am so excited! I am filled with joy about the return and filled with pain because of the separation from my home and family. But Yahweh directs and we will follow.

Your devoted and grateful friend,

Mary

Dear Kathryn, from Anne, an excited Grandmother.

We have just heard from Mary. She wrote and said that she, Joseph, and the boys will be leaving Egypt within the month. Praise God! It has been so long—almost five years—since I have seen my beloved daughter. The last time I saw her, she was heavy with child and going to Bethlehem. Now she returns as the mother of two boys, ages 4 and 1. It is hard to believe.

It has been very difficult to have them gone all this time, and it has affected Joachim's health. So, this news is just the medicine he needs. He will be helping Joseph's father to prepare the house for their return. It needs some minor repairs and a good cleaning, which will be left to Sarah and me, and I'm sure the village women will want to help as well. Our sons are just as excited to have their little sister home again and for all the cousins to meet. We will have a great celebration when they return.

The village was not told much of what had taken place, except that Mary delivered the baby in Bethlehem and there was some danger, so they had to flee to Egypt. When they return, I am sure we will hear more details, but I am not sure what or what not to share. Perhaps, when they come back, you can guide us through the process.

I wanted you to know the news, but, now that I think about it, Mary may have already written to you, or maybe she will be with you shortly. You know how important you have been to our family, and to the lives of many people in Israel. You are God's Prophetess and we depend on you for guidance in many ways. I thank you for your prayers, kindness, and support during these past years, without which I do not think Joachim or I could have survived this ordeal.

You are in our prayers,

Anne

Dear Kathryn, from Joseph, as requested by Mary.

Mary asked that I write to let you know we have safely reached Nazareth. We arrived late in the afternoon ten days ago. The journey itself took thirteen long days.

The boys thought it a grand adventure. They were so excited to see the many caravans we encountered on our way home. Travelers included Jews from all over the world, speaking different languages; people with skin darker than ours, who spoke and dressed differently, playing instruments that were strange to us and even stranger music. There were animals we had never seen before, some tame, some wild. Our little cart, pulled by a burro, paled in comparison, but the boys took turns holding the reins, Joseph Junior sitting on my lap and Jesus sitting next to me. The burro became their pet; they named him Elijah.

Once again, be it Jew or Gentile, we were treated with kindness and support as a young family traveling with two small boys—praise God. The children often were the travelers' entertainment and we shared many meals with those we encountered.

While the trip indeed went smoothly, it was extremely fatiguing for both Mary and me—harder for Mary, I think, because the boys never ran out of energy. They were reluctant to nap while traveling during the day, for fear they would miss something, and when they finally fell asleep at dusk, we both had many chores to get ready for the next day of travel.

When all the chores were completed, Mary and I had a little time to sit and rest. We spoke endlessly about all that had taken place since we left Nazareth for Bethlehem and the census. So many out-of-this-world experiences—it often feels like it was all a dream. But we know, in our minds and hearts, it was Yahweh's plan, always guiding and protecting us.

Our families know bits and pieces of the story and we are unsure how much, when, and with whom we should share, particularly Jesus. We continue to pray about this and will look to Elizabeth and Zechariah for some guidance as well.

The families are delighted to have us home and both sets of parents have aged. I think the worry and uncertainty for our safety and well-being was very difficult for them. It took its toll.

My sisters have families of their own and the cousins had a great time getting acquainted. It was the same with Mary's brothers. About five days ago, the family had a great welcoming feast with the entire village in attendance. Elizabeth, Zechariah, and John were able to attend. John and Jesus took about ten minutes hiding behind their mothers' skirts before they were wrestling and racing through the village. Our two miracle babies. Mary was delighted to have them here, to say the least, and she and Elizabeth spent as much time together as possible after the party and before they left for home.

My parents maintained the house I had purchased for Mary before we left for Bethlehem, so we were able to move in immediately. Mary has been working non-stop to get us settled in and that is why she asked to be excused from writing this letter. She will write once she is settled and rested.

It was so good to see the friends we grew up with here in Nazareth. The village has not changed much, but now my friends all have families of their own and are struggling to provide for them. They tell me that living under Roman rule has gotten worse: increased taxes, cruel retributions for even perceived discontent—there is even talk of rebellion.

Mary has not taken much time yet to visit with her friends, but she is looking forward to that as she gets her second breath. Before I close, let me tell you: Mary may be tired and the mother of two, but she still looks like that beautiful 15-year-old maiden I fell in love with. I daily thank God for the blessing of having Mary as my wife and mother to my children.

We hope this letter finds you well and we are sorry we were unable to stop in Jericho on the way home. You can be assured we will visit you at the first opportunity.

Love,

Mary and Joseph

Dear Kathryn, from Mary, who is home at last.

We have been back in Nazareth a month and are finally settled in. The house is now a home. Joseph has resumed his carpentry work and Jesus follows him around like a little puppy. He loves to go to work with Joseph. He hands him tools, polishes and sweeps as best he can, and asks a thousand questions. He adores Joseph and already wants "to be a carpenter like Abba." He will begin synagogue school next month. I cannot believe it is time for that already.

Baby Joseph spends most of his time with me and he has started walking. We visit both sets of grandparents as often as possible. It feels like we cannot get enough of each other; it has been so long since we have been together. I suppose that will wear off eventually, but I will never again take family or friends for granted.

I spent a few days with Elizabeth when they came for our welcome-home celebration. We had so much to talk about. I missed her so much! John is a beautiful child and he and Jesus became fast friends in that short time. Zechariah looks good for his age and dotes on both Elizabeth and John. We did not get a chance to really talk about what we will tell our sons about their births and all the other miraculous happenings. In a few months we hope to visit them in their home and discuss it.

My friends welcomed me into the community as if I had never left. It brought tears to my eyes when they brought welcoming gifts to the party: household items, toys for the children, and even some things for Joseph and me. It feels so good to be home, but I feel sad and lonesome for the friends we left in Egypt. I know we will never see each other again, but they will always be part of my life and I will pray for them every day.

I cannot wait, when the time is right, to share with my

friends all I have learned about healing. When needed, I hope to be of help to those who suffer with ailments here in the village.

Joseph and I have spoken to both sets of parents about what our families know about the birth of Jesus. They agreed to keep to themselves the messages from Yahweh that we all received, so there is no doubt in the minds of others that Joseph is the father of Jesus. As for our time in Egypt, they were told the truth, that all babies in Bethlehem were in danger from King Herod. His troops were between us and safe passage home, so we fled to Egypt.

When I think of the massacre of those innocent babies and the mothers that died trying to protect them, my heart breaks for the surviving families. How does one cope with this? I imagine one does not. It is their burden for the remaining years of their lives. I pray that Yahweh has brought them some comfort, because no one but Yahweh has the power to ease the pain.

Well, I will end on that sad note. Please remember to pray for those families and their friends who have to live with those horrendous memories.

Love,

Mary

JESUS' PUBLIC LIFE

Dear Kathryn, from Mary, mother of Jesus.

Joseph and I had a terrible fright when we went to Jerusalem for Passover last month. The younger children, as usual, were very excited about going and Jesus was proud to be traveling with the men for the first time, since he is now 12 years old and on the verge of manhood.

All went well until the day we left Jerusalem. We left early in the morning and the caravan was filled with friends, family, and many strangers. At the end of the day, families gathered for the evening meal, but Jesus did not appear. We did not think too much of it at first and sent his brothers to look for him and bring him back for supper. They returned and said they couldn't find him. Then Joseph and my brothers went looking—still no Jesus.

My heart began to race and I was on the verge of tears. Joseph tried to comfort me, "We will find him. We'll head back to Jerusalem in the morning." Needless to say, neither Joseph nor I got much sleep that night and were up while it was still too dark to travel.

I fixed a meal for the children, but neither Joseph nor I could eat anything. We tried not to look upset, so as not to worry the grandparents or the children. I told the children to listen to their grandparents, who would see they got home safely while we began the search.

Anytime we passed someone heading out of Jerusalem, we asked if they had seen a 12-year-old boy and described Jesus, but no one had seen him. By the time we reached the city it was well past sunset, so we found shelter and spent another sleepless night. We started again in the morning, going through the markets, stopping at stalls, asking all the vendors, of any sort, the same question, time and time again, but no one remembered seeing him.

Another night spent in the city—we had a little something

to eat and, after supper, I just broke down and could not quit crying. Poor Joseph! I know he felt the same way, but he is the stalwart one. He had the same look in his eyes as he had when he realized I was ready do deliver Jesus and he would be the one helping me. I tried to remember how well that turned out, but I was terrified.

I imagined all kinds of horrors. Roman soldiers could have taken him for sport, and he could be injured, unable to speak. He could have been attacked by brigands who prey upon the weak and helpless during these festivals. Joseph kept reminding me, "Jesus is in the hands of Yahweh and all will be well." I could hear his words, but my heart did not believe. He held me and I fell asleep, crying in his arms.

The next morning, a sense of doom fell upon both of us as we said our morning prayers, begging for the safe return of our son. We went back to the same area and asked the same questions to people we had not seen before. Around mid-morning, a woman said she heard about a young boy who had been in the Temple with the teachers, who were astounded at the depth of his knowledge and questions. She said people were going to Temple to observe the discussion.

We looked at each other, hoping against hope that it is was Jesus. We had spoken to all the vendors outside the Temple, but did not think to go in. There was a large crowd and we had to push our way in, till we could finally see what was happening.

There was Jesus, sitting with those learned teachers of the word as if he belonged there. I would have collapsed, had Joseph not held onto me. When I steadied myself, we pushed forward further, until we were in the front of the crowd, and I cried out, "Jesus, why have you done this to us? We have been searching for you and feared for your life!"

He stood, looked straight at us, and said, "Why were you looking for me? Did you not know that I must be in my Father's house?"

I could feel Joseph stiffen, and felt the heat from his body. He firmly directed Jesus to come with us, "Now!" and he did.

When we were outside the Temple, Joseph took him by the arm and led us to a quieter area, with me following behind. Joseph was livid; I had never seen him that angry. He took Jesus by the shoulders and said he was never to talk to his mother in such a disrespectful manner again and what was he talking about, his "Father's house"?

"Your father's house is in Nazareth," he continued, "your business is in the carpentry shop. Do you know how much pain you have caused your mother and me? For three days, we did not know if you were alive or dead! You cannot understand this until you have children of your own, and I hope you never have to go through what your mother and I have been through these last three days."

Jesus hung his head and, with tears in his eyes, said he was very sorry he had caused us so much distress.

Just then, some of the rabbis found us and started shouting, "You cannot take this boy! He belongs here in the Temple, to learn. He is gifted and he should stay here in Jerusalem, where we rabbis can nurture that gift."

Joseph was in no mood to talk to them. He made his excuses, took Jesus by one arm and me with the other, and walked us quickly away from them.

All three of us were emotionally fatigued, and I began to cry with relief. Jesus put his arms around me and told me how much he loved me and that he would never be disobedient again. Joseph encircled us with his strong arms and I felt safe and secure as he told us how much he loved us and would give his life to keep us safe.

We had to wait until the next morning to find a caravan in which to travel. So, we went back to the lodgings we had used the previous two nights. We asked Jesus to tell us what had happened and how it happened that he stayed behind.

While in the Temple, he had stayed behind to listen to a debate between two rabbis and, when one of them looked to the audience for support, Jesus spoke up, taking neither side and shared his own opinions. It went on from there, question after question, with Jesus both answering and asking the questions. One of the elders saw that he had no food with him and took him to his own home for meals and to spend the night.

The elder was kind and knew how exhausting it had become for Jesus, so once they left Temple, the questions and discussion stopped. He did ask who his teacher was in Nazareth and about our family. Jesus said he spent time with the children of the household, playing games and telling stories.

We left for Nazareth the next day. That night, after Jesus was asleep, Joseph brought up the topic of Jesus going to Temple school in Jerusalem. Neither of us wanted that to happen—he would be missed too much—but we wanted what was the best for him. We agreed to pray about it and talk with him when we got home.

We arrived on the third day to many relieved faces that had experienced seven days of worry, not just three. There was a lot of scolding and hugging, with his brothers pushing and wrestling. Everyone was so happy to see him.

The next day, we asked what he thought about going to Jerusalem to school and he answered very quickly and said no. He felt that he could learn what he needed here in the Nazareth school, and it is not time for him to leave home. He said he has much to learn from us and he would miss us too much if he left.

What an experience! Another example of trusting Yahweh to take care of those I love. Not to trust is an example of unfaithfulness.

Much love and good wishes,

Mary

Dear Kathryn, from Zechariah, father of John.

Mary, Joseph, and the children have just left for Nazareth. They were here to celebrate Passover with Elizabeth, John, and me. It was a wonderful feast. John and Jesus, who are such good and loyal friends—more like brothers than cousins, were able to spend time alone, roaming the hills of Judah and entertaining the younger cousins in the evening with stories, games, and charades. As an only child, John dearly loves having his cousins here. I think he misses the day-to-day interactions that would happen with siblings. That is why we have made it a point to go to Nazareth as often as possible, and Joseph and his family have done the same in visiting us here in our home.

It was several years ago when the six of us—Joseph, Mary, Jesus, Elizabeth, John, and I—sat down to talk to the boys about their births. Up until that time, we did not go into depth about it. Instead, we chose to do it together, when they were eight years old, as their births were so intertwined.

They listened intently as we told them about the miracle of their births. They asked questions and we answered as best we could. We said we were sure Yahweh has plans for them, although we do not know what they are. We told them they surely were special gifts of God to each of our families, but it might be better if they kept this information to themselves for the time being. They agreed and said, "Is that all?" for they wished to get outside before it became dark. They seemed to take it all with the aplomb that the young have about life, and for a minute I thought they might be thinking we created the story out of our imaginations, for all parents think their children are special.

They have grown to be fine young men and share a deep love for the Word of Yahweh. We have hopes that they both will be teachers of the word someday. John has much fire in his belly. He seems not to tolerate mistreatment of anyone who cannot defend themselves, which has often had him skirting trouble with the Romans, due to his temper. He is a fine student of the law and spends much time with me and the other priests, often surprising us with his questions and opinions. Not all are accepting of him and resent his questions, and sometimes his accusations as well. We have often talked about his behavior and he is always sorry for causing me distress—but not for his deed or action.

Jesus' personality is as day is to night in comparison with John. Jesus is slow to anger and stalwart in demeanor. He has the gift of healing, which we have been doing our best to keep quiet, and is almost as fine a carpenter as Joseph. Both are obvious leaders of the young people in each of their communities. John often incites feelings of anger over injustice, while Jesus speaks in a calm voice, exhorting trust and love for Yahweh.

Kathryn, we pray for your good health daily.

Shalom,

Zechariah

Dear Kathryn, from Jesus, a son who still misses his father.

It soon will be the one-year anniversary of Abba's death and it is a time to recall and honor what a good man my father was. He taught me what it meant to be a man of God, not just in his words, but by his daily example. He was surrounded by his entire family at the moment of his death. He even taught me how to die. He trusted that it was his time. His work here on earth was done and he was ready to return to his creator. It did not mean he loved us any less and wanted to leave us, but that he accepted the plan of God.

He loved all of us with such passion. If he had favorites, he never let any of us know. If the time ever comes that I am to be a father, it is he I would emulate. We were never too old to hug and kiss, his eyes sparkled when he was with family, and how he adored Amma. There was deep love and devotion between the two of them. They touched each other lovingly whenever they were near each other. Except for their age, a stranger might have thought they were newly married. If I ever marry, I would want to be the husband he was.

His other love was his work. He was a master carpenter and people came some distances to purchase a piece of his work or have one commissioned. Those were wonderful days, growing up working in the shop with him. He was patient and playful. We laughed a lot. He made it easy to work with him. His work was another way of honoring Yahweh.

My brothers and I still work in the shop. We produce quality pieces, but they lack the soul of Abba's. When he died, it felt like the soul had left our family as well. He gave us an example to live by, in all areas of his life.

I cried many nights with the pain of losing him. He was my anchor. I went to him with all my doubts and concerns and he listened intently, each and every time, telling me I

82

was a special child of God and to be patient and wait for direction.

Sometimes, just thinking about him brings tears to my eyes because I miss his presence. Other times, remembering his humor or a family member telling a story about him, will make us all smile.

I know it is even harder for Amma. She has lost her soulmate, but she too has a deep faith that all things work together for good. She accepts what is with serenity and love. She is devoted to her family and we have been very blessed with the parents that gave us birth.

I have finished with my schooling. The Rabbi said there is no more he can teach me. If I choose to continue with my education, he says I should go Jerusalem. The thought does not appeal to me. I do not wish to leave my family, but, somewhere deep inside, I know I have other things to accomplish, beyond being a carpenter. But, for now, I am content to stay here, be with family, and work with my brothers in the shop.

Abba will never be forgotten and we all hope we can honor him by the way we conduct our lives.

Please keep my family in your powerful prayers. You are a true healer and woman of God.

Love,

Jesus

Dear Kathryn, from John, son of Zechariah and Elizabeth.

I am preparing to go to the desert to join the Essene community. I have tried to follow in the footsteps of my father, Zechariah, but I feel such frustration with the Sadducees and Pharisees, who are obsessed with the rules and laws of our faith. They think little of the people and their needs. They are power-hungry and I do not think this can be pleasing to Yahweh. I have sat in Temple for many years, listening to their teaching. Many of the rabbis do teach the word of God, but the leaders are prideful and self-serving.

Jesus and I have talked many times about what we should be doing with our lives, which were preordained by Yahweh. Neither of us is sure what path we should take. We both pray daily for direction, so I go to the desert to pray and fast in the hope that more will be revealed to me.

Both my parents are gone, so I have nothing holding me back except my fear of the isolation and the physical hardships. I do believe the voice of Yahweh is directing me to go, so I must obey and trust that all will be well. I hope to tame my impatience and anger, for I cannot understand why people cannot see what I see or hear what I hear. The Jewish people need to prepare for the arrival of the Messiah, to cleanse our minds as well as our bodies, and reawaken the spirit that dwells within.

I have written Jesus to let him know of my plans. I hope it will encourage and support his search for the meaning of his life. He struggles with who he is and what his destiny is. He has the same fears as all of us who ask these questions.

I am asking for your prayers and welcome any thoughts or direction you might care to share with me. I trust your faith and your relationship with Yahweh.

Your servant,

John

Dear Kathryn, from Jesus, a man unsure of his role in life.

While I feel very blessed and dearly loved by my family and friends, I feel a sense of yearning and discontent I cannot explain. My mother chides me about being unmarried: "It is time, since you are well past the age we were wed." It is not that I do not find women appealing and have stirrings in my body, but the commitment of marriage does not seem to be calling me.

Mothers in the village stop by with their marriageable daughters, hoping I will show some interest. I can do that, but I cannot follow up with a betrothal. I know that there is another plan for me, but I know not what that is.

John and I both feel the same way and he recently went to the desert to pray for guidance. Is this something I should be doing as well? John is mighty to behold when he speaks of Yahweh and our need to repent. I believe he has been sent to convert the people and prepare the way for the Messiah.

I do not know my role in any of this and continue to pray for guidance as well. I know I have some healing gifts. I became aware of this as a young man. When someone near me was hurt or in physical distress, I would feel an energy leaving my body. I would touch them and they would be healed. It even happened when someone was in emotional or spiritual distress. I would be drawn to them and they would also be healed. Each time this happened, I asked that they not tell anyone and, for the most part, I think my request has been honored.

I know when holy men come through the village and do healings, it turns into a frenzy and disrupts the daily life of the village. I do not want to be the cause of such a disruption. I do not know why I have been given such a gift, but there are many healers throughout the country. I also know that there have been many women and men in our nation who have been given the gift of wisdom and prophecy and I find it hard to believe I number among their ranks.

Mother and I have been out to the desert to visit John and to bring him food. He tells me my time has not arrived, but the time is close for him to leave the desert and begin his preaching. He says I will know what I should be doing if I listen to the quiet voice of Yahweh.

I have begun to take time regularly to find a quiet place where I can be alone and be still. It does bring me both physical and emotional peace, but I still am not clear about the direction of my life. Maybe I need to follow John into the desert. What do you think?

Your faithful and devoted friend,

Jesus

Dear Kathryn, from Jesus, a surprised miracle worker.

Kathryn, your good friend Jesus is looking to you, an empathetic friend, for support and advice. I remember when, as a young man, I wrote to tell you of the strange experiences I was having—someone would be injured, I would just touch them, and they would be healed. It began slowly, almost by accident. The first time it happened, one of my friends was injured as we were chasing a ball. It looked like he had a badly twisted ankle and, as he was lying on the ground, moaning, I laid my hand on the ankle to keep it from moving. I felt a warm, pulsating sensation flow through my hand and he stopped moaning. When I removed my hand from his ankle, it was no longer twisted.

These incidents—the ability to help people get well, heal injuries, or ease their burdens—began to happen more frequently. At first, it caused me distress. I did not know what was happening and, to this day, I still am not sure. I asked those I helped not to share what happened because I did not want to be treated differently from the other young boys, and I didn't want the responsibility. Still, it became commonplace among my friends to call on me if someone was injured. Then the adults began to call on me, but it certainly did not happen every day—maybe about once or twice a month.

Over time, I became more comfortable with having the ability to heal. But the questions persisted: Why me? How is this going to affect my life? I always thought I would stay in Nazareth and work with my father in the carpenter shop, maybe even be a teacher of the Torah. This healing has caused me to be confused about my role in life and so I prayed daily to be given a sign of some kind. My parents would tell me that I had this gift from Yahweh and my destiny was preordained, but they did not know exactly what that meant. We often prayed, as a family, to be shown the way and the reason.

Last week, my whole family—mother, sisters, brothers—
and many of my close friends all went to the wedding of a
friend's daughter in Cana. We were all excited to be going
since we would get to be with friends and relatives we had not
seen for awhile. My mother was especially excited because
the bride was one of her best friend's daughters.

It was a joyous occasion, with lots of good food, music,
and dancing and, of course, wine. The wine had us singing
and dancing without reservation. We were having a wonderful
time.

Then my mother called me from the dance circle and took
me aside, saying there was no more wine. The family of the
bride was mortified. I said, "So what is it you want me to do?"

"I know not what, just do something," she responded.

I was quite impatient with my mother and spoke more
harshly then I should have. I told her it was not my time, that
it was too public a place and everyone would know and be
talking about it. She nodded her head in agreement and just
looked at me with those eyes that said, "This is my best friend,
please help her." Although I was more than reluctant, I agreed.

As she walked away, I thought about our exchange. Here
I was at a family wedding, having a great time—dancing,
singing, drinking wine—with no responsibilities, no one
asking for help, not being the center of attention. Then my
mother came to me with her request, and that was the end of
being just another guest at the wedding.

She went to the wine steward and told him to do as I
directed. There were some full water jars standing nearby. I
touched and blessed each one and told the wine steward the
wine was ready. He looked at me like I had lost my mind, but
tasted it and said this was a better-quality wine than he had
first served.

The celebration continued long into the night, with more
food to accompany the jars of wine. My mother thanked

me and I apologized for being so sharp with her. I thought that maybe my time has come. Perhaps I will be healing and teaching, not just in Nazareth, but in all of Israel.

Your loyal friend,

Jesus

Dear Kathryn, from an unsettled Jesus.

I had a dream last night. In it, John and I were young and we were having an argument. I cannot remember what it was about, but he accused me of never listening and said, "Do what you want, but I am leaving." I woke calling his name. It has left me unsettled.

I don't know what it all means, but it reminded me of the day our parents told us about our births. We were all in Nazareth for some celebration when my parents called us into our house. We were both angry about it. We were in the middle of a game with the village boys and our side was winning.

They directed us to sit down with a very serious tone of voice. We both complained about being called in and asked if it could not wait until the game was over. Abba said no, in an even firmer voice. Now I started to get worried. What had we done, or what had we not done, that we were supposed to do? John and I looked at each other, shrugged our shoulders, and sat down.

Then, for the next hour or so, they told us about our births. We listened, but it all seemed confusing: angels visiting our parents, our births connected somehow, and we were destined for something, but they did not know what.

When they were finished, they asked if we had any questions. John and I looked at each other and we both said no, still being anxious to get back into the game.

Later that day, when John and I were alone, I asked him what he thought. He said, "I do not know what it all means, but I am not going to worry about it and no one is going to plan my life for me. I will be in charge of my life."

I laughed, because that was and is exactly who John is: always positive about what he believes and moving straight ahead, no matter the obstacles. I wish I could be so positive about what my destiny is. I always envy his determination and his courage to do what he believes is the right thing, no matter the cost.

Please pray for me,
Jesus

Dear Kathryn, from your still-uncertain friend Jesus.

About six weeks ago I went to see my cousin John, who was preaching near the Jordan River. He is indeed a mighty prophet of Yahweh and has gathered many followers. I fear he is in some danger. The Pharisees have questioned him because they see him as a threat to their authority. His message of repentance is needed, and he was baptizing many people that day. I sat and listened to his message and, after he was finished, I approached him and asked to be baptized.

He was reluctant and I assured him it was as the Father wished, and so he did. When he had completed the ritual, he took me aside and said he recognized who I was and what my ministry was to be. I asked him to explain himself because I have been struggling with just those questions myself. He suggested I withdraw to the desert to obtain further clarity on what my role was to be in reforming the Jewish religion. I agreed to the suggestion, bid him goodbye, and told him to be careful.

I agreed so quickly with John's suggestion because when he returned from the desert, he knew exactly what he was to do. He began preaching and gained many converts. I hoped to have the same sense of clarity and direction for my mission. After seeing John, I went back to Nazareth and let my mother and friends know where I was going. Then I left to find the Essenes.

I have been with them all this time. They are very holy men who have dedicated their fasting, silence, and isolation to Yahweh. I lived as they did and had several spiritual experiences. I felt I was being tested and prepared for what was to come.

These are the things I learned. I know I am to remain celibate, to be faithful to the word of God, and to question the rules of our faith practice that get in the way of our relationships with the Father and with our fellow beings here on earth. I learned that Yahweh is a loving Father who accepts all people, especially those that are wounded and broken. I learned that we all have been preordained to take certain roles on earth and it is our job to find out who we really are and what it is we must do to be a manifestation of the Father here on earth. There is so much more but words fail to describe the experience.

It would be so easy to stay here in the desert. It provides a holy atmosphere in which to live and pray, but I know that is not God's plan for me. I leave here in a few days to begin my ministry: to teach, preach, and heal. I am alone, but I know the Father will provide all that I need to accomplish his will. I know this will not be an easy task, but hope my courage will not fail me. You have been a blessing in my life and I know that you will continue to be so.

With grateful love,

Jesus

Dear Kathryn, from Levi, a Galilean tax collector.

Actually, I might better say I was a tax collector. I had been accustomed to being ridiculed, ostracized, and hated by my fellow Jews. It was an easy job. Most people came to me to pay their taxes and if their payments were late, I went to their home, and threatened or humiliated them until they paid. I thought it was worth it, because I was able to make a very good living and able to provide many luxuries for my family. It did not matter to me that I was working for the Romans, collecting taxes from Jews who were usually poor, charging them more than the Romans expected. I cheated even the Romans to have the extra money to support my family.

One day, I was sitting in the booth collecting taxes when a crowd of people started to pass me on the road. I called one over and asked what was happening and he said it was Jesus, the Rabbi from Nazareth. I had heard of him, but never heard him speak or even saw him. I had no interest at all in itinerant preachers, since they had no money at all with which to pay taxes. I went back to working on my ledger.

When I heard someone call out, "Levi, Levi, come, follow me!" I was not sure where the voice was coming from, so I ignored it. Then the crowd parted to let a man walk toward me. He who called out again, "Levi, come follow me." I had no idea who it was until I heard him being called back by the crowd: "Jesus, Jesus." "Oh," I thought, "this must be the Rabbi people have been talking about."

I tried to ignore him, but he kept calling out to me. He approached the tax booth and began to tell me all my sins, then said that I have been forgiven and should come and listen to him preach. His words were so powerful, I closed down the tax booth and joined the crowd.

We went out of town to a small knoll, where Jesus stood

and began to preach. It was as if he was talking to me directly. He spoke of the unconditional love of the Father, that all people were welcomed in his house and no one was excluded. Then, Jesus cured a woman who was hemorrhaging of the curse.

I cannot explain what happened to me. I had such an emotional response to Jesus' words that I wanted to follow him. One of his followers came up to me after he was finished for the day and asked if I was ready to follow Jesus, and I said "Yes, but first I must tell my wife. I will join the group later tonight."

When I returned home and told my wife what had happened and what I wanted to do, she said, "I cannot believe you got religion—you of all people, who only go to Temple on high holy days!" She wanted to know what was going to happen to her and our son. I showed her where I had hidden the money. There was enough if she was willing to be more frugal. She was wailing and cried out, asking how Yahweh could want this of her. I said goodbye to her and my son and left to join Jesus. I did not know why I was chosen, I just knew I must go.

I found out later, shortly after I left the house, that Jesus came and spoke to my wife and son. I do not know what he said, but they both came to the place where his followers were staying to find me and told me they supported me in doing the work of the Lord.

So many things have happened since I have joined this cadre of men following Jesus. They welcomed me into their group like a long-lost brother and, because of my experience handling money, I became the manager of our group's finances.

By the way, I am no longer Levi. Jesus has christened me Matthew

To Kathryn, from the distraught father of James and John.

My heart is so full of pain. My sons, James and John, have left me to follow the Rabbi Jesus.

It all happened so quickly! There were no discussions about it. They heard his words, accepted his call, and they were gone. I begged them not to leave. That did not work, so then I said, "If you leave, you will be dead to me," but they responded, "Abba, it is something we must do." I thought my heart would break. Then, with tears in their eyes, they kissed me goodbye, told me they loved me, and left.

I keep asking myself why. Why did they leave? Why were they so fanatical about this man? Why were they able to leave all that they love: their home, family, the sea, friends—all for what? I have no idea.

Their mother feels differently. She was always ambitious for the boys, wanting them to be more than just fishermen. She says, if what some people say is true, that Jesus is the Messiah, then someday we will have sons who sit in the royal court of Israel. We should be proud that they were chosen for such a great honor.

But this does little to heal the great emptiness in my heart that their leaving has created. I lie awake at night and wish they were here in my home with me. When I wake in the morning, I know that we will not be together, casting the nets, laughing and talking together as we work.

They were more than my sons; they were my comrades. I feel rejected and abandoned. I get angry at Jesus, as well as my sons, for causing me so much distress. Could a man of God cause so much pain, disrupt my life—the only life I know— stealing my sons, and still be a man of God?

My wife, Leah, becomes impatient with me. She says she misses them too, but wants what is best for them. She claims it is not for us to understand God's will. I spend much time thinking and praying about this. I ask Yahweh to deliver me from this anger, relieve this pain, to help me understand and accept, if in truth it be God's will.

I do not want my last words to my sons to be harsh ones, for I will love them until I die. So, I leave tomorrow to seek them out, to hear the words of Jesus, to pray and talk to my sons. Maybe then I will be able to understand and accept.

Your friend,

Zebedee

To my good friend Kathryn, from a confused Nathanael.

I need your wisdom and your guidance. Last week, my friend Philip came to me and said, "Nathanael, we have found the one Moses and the prophets spoke about."

"You mean the Messiah?" I asked. He nodded his head and said, "Yes."

I asked, "Who is this man?"

"Jesus, son of Joseph, from Nazareth," he responded.

I almost laughed out loud. Nazareth! Who or what good has ever come out of that backwater town?

In spite of that, I let Philip persuade me to meet this man. As we approached the area where Jesus was preaching, he stopped speaking, pointed at me, and said to the crowd, "He is a true Israelite. There is no falseness connected to him."

I was stunned. "Do you mean me, sir?" I asked. He nodded yes.

"How can you say anything about me? You do not know me," I responded.

He told me his father knew me. He said he could look into my eyes and see my soul. At that moment, I felt he was a great charlatan trying to impress the crowd.

After he was through preaching, he called me aside and told me things about my life and of my thoughts that no one could possibly know. I was not only amazed, but also very frightened. Was this man in league with the evil one?

Somehow, he knew my thoughts. He smiled and said, "Nathanael, you have been chosen by the Son of Man. You have been blessed by Yahweh and you will do great things." The more he talked, the more frightened I became. Surely he had made a mistake. He wanted me to become one of his disciples.

I decided to stay and listen. He was here in Galilee about

four days. Every day I went to Synagogue and listened to his words—and those words touched my heart.

But how can I do what he asks—leave my family, my home, my work? Am I to leave my life as a scribe to join him and a group of men—which is growing larger every day—to wander the countryside with no place to call home? Surely I can practice what he preaches and stay home here in Galilee.

I have tried all my life to be a good man, but what he asks is too much. I have so many questions: Why did he choose me? Who are these people? What will I be doing? What does he expect of me? Who will take care of my family? How can I just walk away?

I lie in bed at night and cannot sleep. Is my life to become a great mystery? Is this the right thing to do? Is this what the Lord wants of me? I pray, "Oh Yahweh, give me a sign," but I receive no answer.

I am certain now that Jesus is a man of God, a great prophet. He may even be the Messiah. He never makes that claim, but, if he is the Messiah, does that mean I will become a soldier in a rebellion? None of this sounds peaceful or serene, and you know how much I crave these things, as well as my time alone.

You know me well, Kathryn: my need to control, to have structure in my life, to be in charge of my destiny, to know why and how things work or are happening. How will I cope with all the unknowns, and the turmoil of living in community? What if I go, join them, and fail? What if they get to know me and reject me? "What if, what if"—I cannot get these words out of my mind.

Yesterday, I watched Jesus heal someone—a blind man regained his sight. I have never before been witness to a miracle. It has dispelled some of my many fears. I do feel that God is directing me to join Jesus, but will I have the courage? Jesus is putting no pressure on me for an answer. He says, "Take your time, listen to your soul," and assures me that he loves me no matter what I decide.

What do you think I should do, Kathryn? Please help me to decide.

Your friend,

Nathanael

Dear Kathryn, from a rejected and dejected Jesus.

I had been so excited to return to Nazareth, to see my family and the friends of my youth. I expected it would feel so good to be just son, brother, friend, and not leader. I wanted to be loved and accepted for who I am and not for the miracles I perform—a respite from the demands of my mission.

I was welcomed with open arms and heart by my mother, who began to tell me how tired I looked and that I had lost too much weight. Then she and my sister began to make all my favorite foods. I know she worries about me. I can see the strain in her face and the sadness in her eyes. My brothers are as brothers are: noisy, gregarious, teasing, and very pleased to have me in their midst after so long a time.

This visit put a strain on the village, because there were about twenty of us and neighbors opened their homes to my friends, providing both food and shelter. It felt good to sleep indoors, as we often sleep in the open as we travel the countryside.

We had little or no money to offer for this goodwill but my disciples shared the message of the Father, helped with chores, and made themselves useful whenever possible. I am so proud of these men, who have left their family and friends to join me in this holy journey. I know they miss their families and friends as much as I miss mine and yet they go where I go and do what I ask of them, asking only to be part of this great adventure. They are just learning to tap into the grace and power of the Father to heal and preach.

On the Sabbath we went to synagogue. I began to teach and share the message of love and salvation. It was a rude awakening for me. These were people I had known all my life and they took offense. They began to mumble to each other during the service. Finally, one of the elder rabbis stood and asked, "Who are you to presume to know the word of God? We have known you since infancy. Your family lives amongst us. You are no better than any one of us."

I was taken aback and responded, "A prophet is not without honor except in his hometown and among his own kin and in his own house." These were the same people who had welcomed us when we arrived, but were unable to hear the message of God from my lips.

Oh Kathryn, how my heart hurt at that rejection. In other places, people heard and believed and great miracles were able to be performed. But here in my home village, the grace went untapped because of disbelief.

The power is always there, but we have to open our minds and hearts to accept and allow the healing to take place. God freely gives these blessings and people freely accept or refuse it—it is up to them. I came to understand, at a deeper level, that I am just a conduit of that power. I cannot make decisions for another about their response to the message.

When we left the village, I knew it was the last time I would see Nazareth, and I felt very sad.

Blessings and love,

Jesus

To Kathryn, from Rachael, the deserted wife of James ben Zebedee.

I do not understand why I am alone, why I have lost my companion—why James chose Jesus, the rabbi, over me. I am so alone and lonely. My heart aches to have James back here with me. I have asked, I have pleaded, I have cried, I have screamed, "Please come home!" but to no avail.

I married James as a very young woman and left the house of my father, who was a cruel, unloving man. James and the Zebedee clan were the answer to my prayers. We created the loving family I never had, with children who have been loved and valued. And now, just as my father rejected me as his daughter, James has rejected me as his wife.

Deep in my soul, I feel deserving of such treatment and sense I'm being punished for some unknown sin. I feel ashamed. I feel humiliated and, in some ways, I feel diseased. I am sick in mind, soul, and body.

People in the village look at me and wonder what I did or did not do to make James leave. I see them staring at me, or they stop their whispers as I approach. I have suddenly become a different woman since he left. Before, I was Rachael, a woman with a husband and children. Now, I am without a husband. James left me, of his own accord, preferring another life to our life together.

I have lost my identity. I feel unworthy, helpless, and in pain—like a leper, but without the visible signs of disease. People who were once my friends now avoid me, as if to know me is to also become vulnerable to experiencing the same circumstances.

So much happens, on a daily basis, for which I crave love, a kind word, affirmation of a job well done with the children, the meals, the house—but it is not to be. Where is the help I need?

Why did Jesus not ask me what I wanted? Why did he destroy my life?

I have no answers, only questions. The next time they come through the village, I will have many questions for Jesus. In the meantime, I ask for your prayers, for I have much work to do and children to love and care for.

I ask Yahweh every day to return my life to the way it was, or to give me answers as well as the courage and strength to accept what is.

Your very lonely and lost friend,

Rachael

Dear Kathryn, from Susanna, a follower of Jesus of Nazareth.

My heart is so full of love, my soul so full of peace, my mind so full of thoughts of compassion, and my body so full of health and energy. I find myself dancing with joy, hugging strangers, singing out loud, wanting to shout from the roof tops, "I have been healed by the Rabbi Jesus!" I've been healed of my physical ailments, but, more importantly, the "sickness of my soul." I feel boundless energy; the fatigue of a lifetime is gone. I awake in the morning smiling, anticipating the blessings of the day. I have purpose in my life: to be Susanna, the woman Yahweh created me to be. I feel an all-consuming, encompassing love from the Father.

All of this is as a result of meeting the prophet Jesus. Jesus preaches the love of the Father and not the anger of a vengeful God. He tells us of the many blessings we are entitled to as the children of this kind and loving Father. He made me feel valued, respected, protected. He made me laugh, love, and cry with a freedom I have never known before.

I have joined many other Galilean women who accompany him as he travels, preaching and proclaiming the good news of the kingdom of God. In some strange way, we too have become the manifestations of that good news. These women have become my sisters. We accept and love each other just as we are, knowing we are all on the same journey, the journey of self-discovery.

Jesus is strongly criticized, from within and beyond the group, for allowing women to be active among his followers. But he just smiles and says we are a gift from God that cannot be refused, that his disciples have much to learn from us, and there are no castes or divisions in God's kingdom. We are all equal in his eyes.

I hope I have not rambled on and that you can understand

what I have written. I am so excited, and the thoughts come faster than the pen is able to write, but it is most helpful to share with you all that I have experienced and am feeling. I still have much to learn and look forward to the process, because I walk with Jesus every step of the way.

Joanna, Mary the Magdalene, and I send our prayers and love.

Your friend,
Susanna

Dear Kathryn, from Huldah the Healed.

I have overheard the people here in town speak of the many miracles performed by the rabbi, Jesus of Nazareth, and now, praise Yahweh, I have been gifted with one of his miracles.

You recall it has been about 18 years since I was first struck down with my affliction. My back became more bent and twisted as the years went on. Men rejected me because of my appearance.

My family and friends believed I was cursed because of some secret sin, and for a while I believed it myself. But as I thought and thought, and prayed and prayed, I could not recall any sin that would have warranted this kind of punishment.

What I came to believe, and believe deeply, was that this punishment occurred simply because I was Huldah, a woman, a Jewess, a being less valued by my family, friends, and the society in which I lived. Yes, even in the eyes of Yahweh, I was little better than a leper.

As my body became more twisted and deformed, so did my heart and soul. My needs and desires were of no consequence. I was on this earth to be bartered for, to serve whichever man came to own me—and when I lost my ability to serve, to please, to attract, I was worthless. I became repulsive in the eyes of even my family, as I brought shame to the household. I had difficulty breathing. I could no longer look straight ahead, but had to turn my head and body in the direction I wished to see.

Even as I prayed for a miracle, I prayed for revenge against those who abused, rejected, and humiliated me. There was no room for peace or love to dwell within me. I was ugly and unloved. Every day was a burden, to survive without human companionship. The other women avoided me as if I were contagious. I suffered a deep and abiding loneliness, which I knew I deserved.

Then last week, on the Sabbath, I was sitting and begging, in my usual place outside the synagogue, when Jesus came into the courtyard. He was surrounded by many noisy men. He was very still, very quiet, like the eye of a storm. He motioned the men to stay where they were and walked over to me.

I was so bent over, I had to turn my head to the left to see and often sidled along to move from one place to another. He made sure to sit where I could see him easily and held my hand. Looking into my eyes, he began to speak. His eyes were filled with such love. I began to cry as he began to tell me how much he and the Father loved and valued me. He said I was a beautiful daughter of Yahweh and his dear, dear sister. He knew how much I had suffered, both in body and soul. He said that the Father wished for my healing and he was the Father's instrument.

"Your body will be straight and well," he said, "but, more importantly, your soul will be healed. You will experience love as you never have before. You will feel valued, respected, and joyful. You will stand tall, able to see the goodness in all things, as well as yourself. Today is the birth of the true Huldah," he concluded.

Then he stood, put his hand on my head, and said, "Huldah, you are set free of all your infirmities." I stood at once. Standing erect for the first time in 18 years, I was able to take a deep breath and looked directly into those loving, intense, deep brown eyes.

Praising Yahweh amidst tears of joy, I walked around the courtyard, testing my healed body. How light I felt! I danced and sang, as a wellspring of happiness bubbled within. I looked at the people in the courtyard and, where I once saw the enemy, I now saw the glow of goodness and love.

Jesus walked over to me and held me in a long, tender embrace, then whispered, "There will be another who will love you as I do. That man will manifest the Father's love to you for all your life. You have much to give, as you have suffered much, and you too will become an instrument of Yahweh's healing and love."

To think, Kathryn, that I did not even need to ask Jesus for this miracle! He gave it freely, out of his love for me. I have told this story many times in the last week, but I wanted especially to share it with you. You were always supportive and loving toward me. Even in the depth of my ugliness, you saw beauty.

Thank you, kind Kathryn, with much love,

Huldah

Dear Kathryn, from your grief-stricken friend Mary.

I have just learned of the gruesome death of my dear cousin John, the only child of Elizabeth and Zechariah. John was beheaded and his head was presented to Herod on a platter at a celebration in his palace. While I miss Elizabeth every day, I am grateful for God's mercy in taking her and Zechariah before their beloved son was murdered.

John brought so much joy and pleasure to his parents. He was a good friend to us and brother to Jesus. Joseph and I took much delight in his growing-up years. He often stayed with us and Jesus went to Judah and stayed with his family.

John was an intense boy and an even more passionate young man. He loved Yahweh, his family, animals, and the land. He ached for the injustices of the world. He believed he was called to preach, to teach our people a new way of worshipping God. He felt in his soul the Messiah's impending arrival.

Before he started that mission, he lived in the desert, fasting and praying for a very long time. By that time his parents were gone, so Jesus and I would go to visit and bring him gifts of food and words of encouragement.

I cannot even imagine the pain of losing a child, much less having one murdered, ripped from your life for doing God's will. Please God, it will never happen to me, for that would be something I could not bear. A child should be at their parents' deathbed and I pray that Jesus will attend me at my death, just as he and I were with Joseph when he died. Joseph died in our arms, peaceful in our love. It allowed us to release him into the arms of the Creator. I pray for the same kind of passing.

John was alone and with those who hated him when he died, but I am sure his parents stood with the Almighty to welcome him home. But I wonder if, even in the afterlife, could a parent be free of the pain of their son's brutal murder, the ending of such a young life?

John was a lion of Yahweh. He roared the truth, challenging our faith. He was a prophet of God. Was anyone listening?

Let us both pray for our children, that their lives be long, filled with joy and peace, and that their children will be at their side in the time of their passing.

Love,

Mary

Dear Kathryn, from Mary of Magdala, a follower—at a distance—of the Rabbi Jesus.

The Rabbi Jesus recently came to speak and I need to share my thoughts and fears with someone. It is hard for me to believe everything Jesus says because it is too good to be true. I began to follow him, but stayed in the background, never approaching or talking to any of the people who were in attendance. But one of the women in his group—her name was Joanna—noticed me and I spoke with her about my fear and distrust of men. I did not want to tell her my whole story. She suggested I write to you.

Let me tell you who I am. I grew up in a home with a violent father who was very abusive to all of the children. My mother tried to intervene, but also felt the wrath of his anger. When I came of age, he sold me to a man who was thirty years older than me. There was no marriage ceremony because I was a commodity being sold and then bought. Our first night together was a nightmare. I was bruised and bloodied. We moved to a village very far from my family. Shortly after arriving, he began to sell me to other men for sexual favors.

I became like a dead person, lying there unresponsive, not ever speaking. My only wish was to die. I prayed to Yahweh to make this happen, but evidently my punishment, for whatever sin I committed as a child, still had not been atoned. Of course, I was shunned by the women in the village and was not allowed in the synagogue, as I was considered unclean, like a leper.

This went on for several years until, suddenly, the man died. I cried with happiness, praised Yahweh, and began to plan my new life. But nothing had changed. I had no family, no friends, no way to support myself, so I was forced to resume my prior profession to have money for food and shelter. I still cried at night, asking what I had done to deserve this, but no answer came.

I spent time around the marketplace, soliciting business, when I began to hear talk about the Rabbi Jesus. They said his message was about love, acceptance, and forgiveness. He ate with moneychangers, beggars, tax collectors, Samaritans, and even lepers. I thought, "I need to go see this man."

The first time I saw him, he healed a woman who was so bent over she could not see in front of her and had to sidle when she walked. Jesus spent some time with her and, the next thing we knew, she stood erect and, raising her eyes to the heavens, she thanked Yahweh. I was not that impressed because there are many miracle workers in these villages. They come, they go. I was impressed with the gentle way Jesus spoke and his love for the little ones, often calling for the children to come close. When he said he came, not for righteous, but for the sinners, I felt he was speaking to me.

I can continue to follow him as he travels, as I have saved some shekels and am able to provide for myself. But my fear is that my reputation will follow me and Joanna will reject me and tell others. She said you know Jesus. She said you are a wise woman, blessed by God, who helps all who ask. I am asking. I long to be among his followers, but fear rejection. Any wisdom you wish to share will be appreciated.

Shalom,

Mary Magdalene

To Kathryn, from Ezra, as written at the behest of his friend Aaron. I hope you can help him.

Kathryn, the young rabbi Jesus was here in Bethsaida several months ago, preaching in the synagogue. While he was here, he healed my blindness, returned my sight. My friends Jacob and Aaron had led me to Jesus and begged him to cure my blindness. Jesus told everyone to stay behind, then took me by the arm and led me outside of the city. He spoke to me of God's great love for me and asked if I truly desired this healing. Of course, I answered, "Yes, Rabbi."

We sat beneath some trees that gave us shade. It was pleasantly cool. I could feel a soft breeze, smell the nearby cedars, heard the singing of the birds. He continued, "Many are blind who can see." He wished for me the clear vision that comes from the soul.

He told me he would describe what he was doing during the healing so that I would not be anxious and could relax. He prayed aloud, asking his father for direction and guidance: "Use my hands as an instrument to heal your servant Ezra. Manifest your powerful but gentle healing energy during this time."

He moved his hands around my head, not touching me. I felt the movement even before he explained what he was doing. He then spit into his hands, gently rubbed the spittle on my eyes, and laid both hands across my eyes for several minutes, all the while humming to himself.

Eventually, he removed his hands and asked if I could see. I rubbed my eyes, looked around, and saw forms or shadows and their movements. He repeated the entire process and, when I rubbed my eyes for the second time, I could see clearly.

The sun hurt my eyes, and colors were so bright they took my breath away. I looked upon the face of Jesus, the holy man, the son of God, this healer who took pity on me and cured me. Tears came to my eyes, I began to sob, and Jesus held me, stroked my head, and rocked me while continuing to hum. When I had stopped crying, he and I both said prayers of thanksgiving and praise. He then ordered me not to return to town, but to go directly home.

I was euphoric for several weeks, feeling like a special son of God and very blessed. It was what I had prayed for, this oh, so many years. During that time, I did very little except to repeat the story of the healing to the people of my town. In fact, I told the story so often I began to feel resentful whenever I was asked to repeat it.

I did very little besides talk because I did not know what to do. Many questions have come into my mind. How does a man with vision live? Why was I chosen? What am I to see with my restored vision?

I began to see the ugliness of the world as well as the beauty. Anxiety raised its ugly head. What if the cure did not last? Being sighted made new demands upon me and I had no idea how to respond. I began to doubt. I began to feel I do not deserve this miracle. Every morning, I wake up and, before I open my eyes, I wonder, "Is this the morning my sight will be taken from me?" My vision has begun to blur; is it because of my anxiety or is it the beginning of the end?

My family and friends grow impatient with me, and who can blame them? I grow impatient with myself. Sometimes the confusion and fear become so intense I wish for the safety of the darkness.

I feel like I am going mad. Is this not what I wished and prayed for, since the blindness struck me as a child? I begged for it, pleaded with God, "Please let me see again." And now that I can see, I feel my vision has become a burden, not a blessing. What is it that I am so afraid to see? Where is the clear vision that comes from the soul?

I need your help Kathryn. I await your reply.

Your servant,

Ezra

Dear Kathryn, from Mary of Magdala, a committed follower of Jesus.

It has been about six months since you encouraged me to speak to Jesus directly. It took me awhile to gather my courage, which was strange for me, since I had the reputation of being afraid of nothing and no one. I guess I created that persona so people would be wary of trying to take advantage of me or hurting me in some way.

In my mind, I practiced over and over how I would tell him about my life and how sorry I was for the things I had done. I had told no one among his followers, but I think some of the women suspected, because they were very cool toward me. I had no idea how he would react to my story and I was fearful of being rejected.

Well, one evening when Jesus was alone and separated from the main group, I approached him. He was sitting under a tree, facing away from the path I was on. I did not want to startle him and made some noise as I neared him so he would know someone was coming.

Without turning around, he said, "Mary why has it taken you so long to come to me? I have been waiting for you." Then he stood up, turned around to face me, opened his arms wide, and said, "Come." I raced into his arms and, as he held me, I began to cry as I have never cried before. I do not know how long I sobbed, but Jesus held me, saying nothing, until I was able to stop crying.

When I stopped, he wiped my face with his mantle and invited me to sit under the tree with him. Then he began speaking. He told me the story of my life, from the time I was a child until that very day. He knew the smallest details of my life: where I hid when my father was in a rage, what my favorite foods were, the shame I bore, the guilt I felt—he knew everything. I was relieved of the trauma of having to tell my own story. What a blessing!

He then looked at me and asked, "What is it you ask of me?" I told him I wanted to be one of his followers. I wanted to be forgiven for my sins. I wanted to be worthy of his love and be of use to him.

He replied that I have always been worthy of his love. My sins were forgiven. I was to be a great help to him in his mission. He said I will be respected and admired as one of his most intimate followers. "How is that to be?" I asked. "It is not necessary for you to know the answer to that question. Just have faith and accept my words as the words of Yahweh," he replied.

We returned to the main encampment and he asked everyone to gather around. Then he introduced me as a new member of the assembly. He said I was to be welcomed, treated as a sister to all, and that I had been sorely wounded and needed time to heal. "She was lost, and now is found."

People immediately came forward, men and women alike, to welcome me. The tears started again and the women led me back to their area of the camp and offered me support with such tenderness that I was unable to stop the tears. They literally put me to bed and one of them slept next to me in the event I woke and needed something during the night.

I have begun a great spiritual journey and continue to learn and grow every day. I feel so blessed to be among the chosen and do everything I can to be an example of Jesus' teachings.

Thank you so much for your help in the past. I keep you in my prayers.

Love,

Mary Magdalene

Dear Kathryn, from Veronica, a follower of Jesus the Rabbi.

It was very good of you to ask my sister Miriam about my health and activities. I have been with the women that follow the Rabbi Jesus for over a year now. There are about forty of us, young and old, wives, widows, maidens, and mothers with small children, which number seven, four boys and three girls. We have become like family; these children have more mothers than they bargained for. We cook, wash clothes, tend the ill or injured, and maintain order out of what could otherwise be chaos. We offer these services not only to our own group but also to all who come to hear the words spoken by Jesus. We work very hard, for long periods of time.

I'll share one day that I will never forget. We were walking along the seaside, and more and more people were joining the walk. It seemed we numbered in the thousands. We were beginning to get anxious—how were we to provide food and drink for so many? What if they turned on us? Jesus seemed oblivious to all of this. He moved off the beach and walked up to the top of a gentle, slopping hill. The people followed. They were moving up and down the knolls and crevasses of the green hillside, looking for spots to sit. There were so many people that some had to stay on the beach.

Jesus stood on the crest of the hill, raised his hands, and all was quiet as they sat where they could. His voice carried on the wind, straight on to the sea, so all heard every word. He spoke of the love the Father has for us, the need to forgive others as we have been forgiven, the absolute necessity to love one another as he loves us. The crowd was very still, listening intently. Even the children were not restless.

He spoke at length and, as dusk approached, he called a few of us to him and said, "My people hunger and thirst. We must feed them." Someone asked, "How can this be done? All we have are five loaves and a few fish." He asked that the bread and the fish be brought to him. He blessed the food, broke the loaves, and gave them to us. We continued to break the bread and the fish into pieces as we walked among the crowd, distributing food to the throng.

Judas said the crowd numbered more than 4,000 and you know how good he is with numbers. It took several hours to feed everyone and we never ran out of food. In fact, we were left with seven baskets of bread and fish. The magnitude of this miracle took our breath away. The crowd began to call out, "Hail Jesus, King of the Jews!" At that point, the men spirited him to safety lest the crowd injure him in their enthusiasm.

The men in our group grow more excited every day, hoping the people will rise up, overthrow the Romans, and crown Jesus as King of Israel. I have no idea if this is going to happen, or if is even meant to be. What I do know is that Jesus is a peace-loving man. I have never heard him utter a violent word, except when he threw the moneychangers out of the Temple. I also know he was sent from God, because he has great powers to heal and preach. He accepts all he meets—sinners, lepers, gentiles, Romans, Samaritans, even women and children—with open arms and great affection.

As usual, we women were left to clean up. I do not have the strength I once had, but I do as much as I can. Everyone accepts our weaknesses and failings and the younger women are often left to tend we older women, as well as the others.

We talked of this miracle well into the night and pondered many things, including the possibility that the men are right: Jesus is the Messiah and will lead the Jewish people out of bondage.

I thank you for your prayers. It's clear you have many supporters and people praying for you among the followers of Jesus.

Shalom,

Veronica

Dear Kathryn, from Leah, follower of Jesus the Rabbi.

Good news! Mary, the mother of Jesus, has come to visit. She arrived several days ago. We were all surprised, pleased, and excited, since we were not expecting her—Jesus most of all. It is a real blessing for him. He is always more relaxed and energetic during her visits. I am sure it is from the love, support, and nurturing he receives.

At this time, we are encamped outside of Gennesaret and we have so many new followers that we struggle to find them all a place to sleep. But, at her request, Mary has stayed with us women, in very rustic conditions, both at night and when she is not with Jesus during daylight hours.

During those times, some of our entourage would gather at the women's camp, waiting for her return. It is well known that Jesus has never denied any request from his mother. Consequently, people have come with pleas and favors, begging her intercession with her son.

She begins each interaction with the holding of hands and a prayer to Yahweh for guidance. It is interesting to watch as she sits quietly and listens intently, focusing only on the person speaking and seemingly oblivious to any activity taking place around her. She speaks only to ask a clarifying question. Her presence radiates love, compassion, and empathy.

She never responds immediately, but bows her head—I assume in prayer—to discern the will of the Father. Her responses are thoughtful and wise. Often, they solve the problem with no needed interaction with Jesus. Even when, in her gentle way, she takes someone to task for being selfish or self-serving and directs them to ask Yahweh for forgiveness and humility, they never feel chastised. It is a wonder to behold.

Yesterday, we were all listening to Jesus preach, including Mary. There was an exceptionally large crowd. When we first arrived, we found hordes of people waiting for us, and they had brought their sick to be healed. Many, many people were healed when Jesus laid hands on them. Some just touched his cloak and they too were healed. You can imagine how the word had spread through the countryside after so many healings, thus accounting for the great numbers listening to him preach that day.

Jesus spoke of the fallacy of the rituals of cleansing and restrictions around food and eating. "The time has come to stop deluding yourselves that we are doing the will of Yahweh with these practices." He was condemning what we believed to be a commandment from God, which we have practiced for hundreds of years.

"It is not what you put in your mouth that cleanses or defiles you. It is what is in your heart. From your heart you can produce evil, such as murder, envy, slander, pride, adultery, wickedness, or deceit, which defile, or you can practice love, feed the hungry, visit the sick, and care for the young and aged. These loving actions affirm the word of Yahweh."

There was much mumbling among the crowd and, as usual, the Pharisees were the most vocal, accusing him of being an unfaithful Jew. He repeated, "Love is the answer to all questions."

Then, to all our surprise, Mary stood and everyone became still. We could see the shock on her face. Mary, a truly holy woman and faithful Jew, asked the question most of us were thinking but lacked the courage to ask. "My son, can we not do both: continue the rituals that my mother taught me as her mother taught her, going back through the many generations of our people? These rituals bring me comfort and connection to my ancestors. I would feel bereft and empty without them in my life. Can we not do both—continue the practice of our ancestors and also practice love and the good works that love produces?"

"My beloved mother, I thank you for your love and your loved-filled question," Jesus responded. "I also know you are a woman who does practice both, but if you continue the practice of these rituals, you are fooling yourself that you are doing the will of God. The Father asks for the spirit of the law, not the letter. There is nothing wrong in the washing of foods and hands before we cook or eat; it is a healthy thing to do. Yahweh is neither pleased nor displeased. It is a false concept that has become a habit. Yahweh often asks of us that which is difficult or uncomfortable. You will find peace and solace knowing you are a woman taking this difficult step, which will allow you to have a deeper and more meaningful relationship with the Father and with all those whose lives you touch."

Then he continued, "It is as if the rituals are comfortable, like worn out old shoes. They no longer serve the purpose to protect and warm your feet. Then, when a beloved brings you new shoes that are not only just as comfortable but keep your feet from injury and the cold, and yet you are unable or unwilling to throw out the old shoes."

We women talked well into the night about all that was said. We all agreed how difficult it would be to give up the familiar in our lives, and not just the rituals. We all agreed there were times the familiar could be painful or cause distress and that Jesus continues to ask for transformation, not just change.

We went to our beds wondering how many old shoes we had in our closets.

A beloved Servant of Jesus and your friend,

Leah

Dear Kathryn, from Anna, who used to love food more than anything.

Let me tell you of my miracle. For a very long time I had been filled with fear, dread, and anxiety. Age is the culprit—my mental acuity and physical strength are slipping away. I have looked at my reflection in the mirror and now see a woman I barely recognize. My once thick, lustrous, dark hair now hangs limp and gray. Where there was smooth, glowing skin, there are wrinkles. My hands hurt, and my arms and legs have lost the strength I once had. I once was a very strong woman and proud of it.

But, for all of that, I worry not about how I look, but about my inability to earn a living weaving, and that I will live beyond the time the few shekels I have saved can support me. I have no one to support me or depend on. I thought, "What is to become of me?"

Money was in my every thought: how to earn it, how to spend it, how to save it. I worried late into the evening, causing sleepless nights which led to problems during the day. I felt abandoned, unloved, without energy to face each day, my life drained.

All I had in my life was food. After all, food is good for us. We have to eat. Then I started to hoard and hide food, lest someone stop to visit and I would feel obligated to share. Food became my true friend and companion. I prayed for a miracle— what kind of miracle, I knew not. Was it for money? Was it for more food in the house? Was it to be young again? There was no miracle, no sign or direction. I hid in the house, isolating myself, with my only consolation being eating in secret.

My bossy friend Diana who was always trying to get me out of the house, insisted I go with her to see a young rabbi who had recently arrived in town. Diana said, "Something is going on.

123

People are gathered around the house where he is staying and we should go and find out what is happening." You know how nosy she is. She said, "It will get your mind off your troubles."

So, I went. I thought I had no choice, since she is so controlling. She also knows me—she had brought me sweet breads to coax me out of the house.

We walked to the house where the rabbi was. When we arrived, there were about fifteen or twenty people—men, women, and children—some standing, some sitting in the shade of nearby trees. They seemed subdued in some way, anxious or expectant—I am not sure which. The children were busy being children, chasing, jumping, laughing, and squealing in delight.

Every now and then, someone would exit the house and a man who seemed to be in charge would call out the name of another person who would then go into the house. Most of the adults would rush to the exiting person and start questioning them, so we did too. "What happened? Have you been cured? What did he say? What did he tell you?"

It sounded to me like this Jesus is a fake of some kind. People are so gullible. He had them believing he knew their past, knew their innermost thoughts and secrets, and could predict the future. "What fools!" I thought. I asked the man how much he charged, and he said nothing. "What does he want for his services?" I asked, and he responded, "Nothing; only that they be happy."

Everyone who came out mentioned forgiveness or trust, words people bandy about all the time and then continue to live as before. The future was what I wanted to know. I knew he was a fake, but part of me wanted to believe. What could it hurt? It was free. Diana encouraged me to give my name to one of his followers outside the house, but I resisted. I needed time to think about it.

I do not know how long we stood there. I think two more people had gone in, with the same scenario when they came out, and I told Diana it was about time to go home. Diana said, "Not yet. Go, give them your name."

Just then, the man came to the door and said, "Anna." I thought there must be another Anna in the group, but no one moved. He called again, and no one moved.

I walked up to the man and said, "My name is Anna, but there must be some mistake. I made no request to see the rabbi."

"Jesus makes no mistakes. He responds to needs, not requests," he said, and motioned me to follow him into the house.

There were two women and three men in the house. I did not know which of the men was the rabbi. One of the men approached me, greeted me by name, took my hand, and said, "Come, follow me."

He took me to a corner of the room, where there were two stools facing each other. He sat in one, with his back facing the rest of the room. I sat in the other and started to explain that there must be some kind of mistake.

He interrupted me and said, "Be still, my beloved sister, and listen. The miracle you have been praying for is about to happen." He spoke so quietly and, with his back to the others I knew only I could hear him. He then spoke of my life, told the story of my birth, spoke about my dead relatives by name. He even knew the color of the first shawl I wove. He spoke of my present terrors and knew of my secret eating.

At first, I was very frightened. I thought, "Who is this man—an evil conjurer?" He said to me, "No, Anna, I do not come from the evil one. I come from Yahweh." My immediate thought was, "How do you know what I'm thinking?!"

He then addressed every one of my fears, one by one, asking, "When did you lack for anything?" I knew he was a holy man when he continued, "My father is your father, the creator of all things. He has protected and cared for you the whole of your life. You have no need to know the future because our father

125

will continue to protect and care for you in the future just as he has done in the past."

Jesus spoke of love, compassion, honesty, forgiveness, and acceptance. He told me I could be of service to our father by caring for the poor and the needy, that my life begins today if I will accept and trust in him. I will no longer be alone, I will no longer turn to food for love and compassion, I will have all that I need in abundance—enough to share with all that come to me for help—if I respond with love, acceptance, and compassion. I responded, with all my heart, "Yes, Jesus!"

I felt all my fears melt and leave my body with each exhalation. I felt I was a new woman, ready for my new life, whatever it may bring. "Now you can speak," he said, but I had no words, only cleansing tears that turned into sobs of relief and gratitude. He held me in his arms until the crying subsided, then led me to the door and said, "Go forth and be well. You are healed."

As I stepped out of the house, I was blinded by the sunlight for a moment. Some of the people rushed toward me. I thought I might swoon from it all, but dear Diana was right there to support me, giving the crowd orders to move back and let me be. Even after she let me rest in the shade for a while, I could not speak, even to Diana. We then slowly walked home. Diana asked me no questions, other than whether there was anything I needed. She put me to bed and I slept.

When I woke, Diana was sitting near me, doing some needlework. I told her the whole story, just as I am telling you. I have much to ponder and much to learn. I look forward to the future with great appreciation and awe. Peace and joy have come to my house and I have opened the door to welcome them in. Glory to God in the highest!

Love and Shalom,

Anna

Dear Kathryn, from Jesus, your overwhelmed friend.

It has been some time since I have written, but feeling overwhelmed and discouraged is always a motivator for me. Even as I sit down to write this letter, I feel impotent and overwhelmed in dealing with my responsibilities, followers, family, friends, and enemies. I think, "I did not choose this life. Why me?" A recurrent theme these last few years. How I long for the simple life I had in Nazareth with my family. These moods come upon me periodically and I know they will pass, but they are difficult to endure. One of the things that does help me is writing or talking to you.

My dear Kathryn, you are such a shining example of acceptance and loving patience as you live with your infirmities, open to the will of the Father under all circumstances. I think of you often and wonder, "What would Kathryn do in this or that circumstance?"

My followers grow in numbers daily and I wonder how I will provide for them. They are like children, looking to me for all their physical, spiritual, and emotional needs. They are so many and I am just one man. They do not seem to understand that I am but the messenger, and yet I often doubt my ability to convey the message.

My trust in Yahweh never wavers; it is me I do not always trust. I think I am speaking clearly to my followers while I preach, but the questions they ask, the conversations they have with each other, prove that I am saying one thing and they are hearing another. The petty jealousies, the arguing, the jockeying for position, all add to my discouragement. These times are episodic and short-lived, but I continue to wonder why they have to occur at all.

I continually seek to do Yahweh's will in everything and it feels like I'm not enough. I feel I am not measuring up, but I know my God is a loving God, not a vengeful, punishing God.

I feel lonely in the midst of the group, my energy drained. I am encompassed by an emotional and physical fatigue and have the need to withdraw, to be alone, to pray and rest. In these times of isolation and prayer, the message that often comes to me is, "Stop trying to be perfect. Only God is perfect. Accept what is. Depend on Yahweh and all will be well." That soothes my soul, refreshes my mind and body, allowing me to begin the work of my Father anew.

Thank you for listening,

Jesus

Dear Kathryn, from Esther, a faithful servant of Jesus.

Things do not go well. I wonder if I have made a mistake in joining the followers of the Rabbi Jesus. I had such high hopes, was so moved by his words and touched by his energy that I chose to leave all that was familiar and dear to me. I had a deep desire to be physically close to him, to be part of a community that loves, supports, and serves him. So, a month ago, I became part of the group of women that travel with him and his disciples.

Being a newcomer, I was given the menial jobs—cleaning up after meals, running errands, keeping the camp area clean and neat. I learned very quickly that I was to be seen and not heard. I was not to question, but only to obey. A few of the women were welcoming and helpful, but most were not. I asked questions, made helpful suggestions on how things could be done faster or better, but they did not appreciate the feedback. The women in charge only wanted me to do the work that was assigned to me and keep my mouth closed. I think they would like me to leave. What happen to "love your neighbors" and accepting each other as daughters of Yahweh?

I felt so frustrated and disappointed, I went to Jesus and spoke to him of my problems. He listened with his whole body, his gaze on me the entire time. I felt so loved and respected. He said, "My dear, beloved Esther, my Father has known you for all time. He knows you as intimately as a husband knows his wife. He knows your strengths, which are many, and he knows your sins. He loves you for both because that is what makes you Esther."

Then he continued, "You have come to this imperfect place because of your love for me. Now is the time for you to learn to become the woman the Father intended you to be—not a perfect woman, but a complete woman. Every woman here has to learn this. You are living through their learning process too. Listen to your inner voice. Experience and accept yourself as you are, not as you wish to be. You bring much to the community and, in accepting the divine that dwells within, and your imperfect state, you will see others with different eyes. You will see reality though the eyes of divine love."

As you can see, Kathryn, I have much to learn, much to experience, so I plan on staying and hope to see truth and not my imperfect reality. I will let you know how my journey to completeness progresses.

Peace, joy, and good health,

Esther

Dear Kathryn, from Philip, a conflicted follower of Jesus.

It seems only a short time ago that Jesus came into the village of Bethsaida and spoke in the synagogue, but in reality it has been almost three years. He spoke so eloquently, with so much truth and wisdom. He spoke of a gentle, loving God, a God who was not vengeful, who was not to be feared. He spoke of the dangers of becoming obsessed with rules and power. He spoke of loving one another as we love ourselves and he spoke of the hypocrisy of some of the Jewish leaders. It was as if he had spoken directly to me. My heart opened to his words, but my mind struggled with their meaning. I did not understand every word he uttered, but, in some strange way, I believed everything he said.

When he spoke, his voice was so quiet, so gentle, you had to strain to hear him. Nonetheless, the words seemed to vibrate within my body. He moved with such grace, slowly, using his movements to emphasize certain phrases or words. It felt neither planned nor staged.

There was a pale, golden light that often surrounded him, which followed him as he moved about. I asked my friend Levi, who was sitting next to me, if he saw the light. He looked at me strangely and asked, "What light?" I still see the light at times when Jesus is teaching or healing.

I listened as he spoke, wishing it would never end. I had tears in my eyes, my heart was racing, and I felt feverish. It was as if my daily prayer, "Yahweh, help me to become the man you want me to be," was answered. This was the way, the way of Jesus.

I was the last person left in the courtyard after Jesus finished speaking. I sat, as if in a hypnotic state, unable to move, my body still but my mind rushing about, filled with questions. "What does all of this mean? Will I get to hear Jesus speak again? Why was I so impressed when others seemed only mildly interested in what he had to say? How will this change my life?" Suddenly I felt a hand on my shoulder and sensed such a rush of energy throughout my body from the touch that I almost fell over.

There was Jesus, standing there, looking at me with a smile on his face. I will never forget his words: "Peace be with you, Philip. I have come for you. You are a beloved son of God and have been chosen to be with the son of man."

"Yes, master, I will join you," I responded, so quickly, even though I did not know what it all meant. All I knew was that I wanted to be with this holy man, to learn from him, to serve him. Little did I guess what was to come. It was later in the day that I became anxious and questioned the wisdom of my actions. "What about my rabbinical studies? What about my parents, whom I help support? What about Judith, my betrothed?"

Jesus introduced me to several of his friends and they laughed and teased me about having "the look." They led me to the area where they had camped for the night. The look they were talking about was the dazed and bewildered look on my face, and yet I felt euphoric. I would see that same look many times on the faces of the men Jesus later called to be among his followers.

After our evening meal, Jesus retired to an area some distance from the main camp—his usual custom, as I later learned. Five of us sat around the fire, talking, mostly with me listening. All had some variation of my experience in meeting Jesus. They spoke of their concerns, fears, and even guilt about leaving family, friends, and responsibilities to follow this itinerant rabbi. They suggested that in the morning I should make my intentions known to all who were important in my life. It would not be easy, and one of them would accompany me if I so desired.

I chose to do it alone. I did not want my family and friends to think I was under duress or being forced in some way. It was the hardest thing I have ever done. I had no answers to my family's questions: "Why are you leaving? When will you return? Where are you going? What will you be doing? Who are these men?" I just kept repeating, "I do not know, I do not know. I just know that I have to be with Jesus."

And Kathryn, to this day, after almost three years, I am not always sure of the answers to these questions. I still do not always understand what he is saying or teaching. The one thing I do know is I love him more every passing day and have a deep desire to be his faithful follower.

There are many men and even some women who travel with Jesus, but there are twelve of us, most of us strangers to each other in the beginning, whom Jesus calls his disciples. The twelve of us have become like family, brothers, with all that implies. The politics of family, sibling rivalry, bickering, jealousies all occur, as well as the deep love, loyalty, and support we give to one another.

I will not use any names to accuse or judge, for I am as guilty as the rest. It gets very wearing, trying to suppress my feelings of impatience and irritation. I can speak to no other about this, for fear of undermining the work of Jesus or appearing disloyal. You are the one person who will listen, understand without judgment, and who appreciates the need to speak of these feelings to better understand my emotional state. So, here goes.

At times, we are rude to each other, headstrong, demanding, judgmental, bigoted, gluttonous, arrogant, miserly, slovenly, irresponsible, wasteful, lazy, self-centered, and even violent. What was Jesus thinking when he chose such a group of flawed, imperfect human beings to be his apostles?

Jesus is our leader, and often forced by our behavior to act as a stern, loving father and peacemaker. Other times, he steps back and lets us work out the conflict ourselves. Our behavior never seems to diminish the love and confidence he has for us, but I think it can get very discouraging for him. I know how distressing it is for me. During those times, all I want to do is escape from the group and quit it all. Jesus reminds us constantly to look to ourselves, to look into our hearts, to learn who we are, to learn we cannot see through the distortion of our own reality. I am still trying to sort this out and practice what he preaches. It is not easy.

But, for all of that, these men are capable of such great love, kindness, tenderness, loyalty, bravery, and singlemindedness of purpose in serving Jesus. We have among us men with brilliant minds, some who are craftsmen, fishermen, tradesmen, some have great physical strength, some organizing skills, others are wise in the ways of the world. I could go on and on about the diverse gifts these men bring to our group. Our strengths as well as our weaknesses are being used in the service of Yahweh. Jesus often reminds us that our learning and discernment come from our weaknesses, discomfort, and pain; little is learned from pleasure and joy. We should learn to be grateful for the blessings of conflict, pain, or distress—another difficult lesson to learn.

I guess I have answered my own question about why Jesus chose such flawed and imperfect human beings. The answer is that there is no other kind. The miracle is, he is still able to use us for the honor and glory of Yahweh. We have traveled many miles in the last three years and will be in Jerusalem for Passover in a few days.

Jesus says his time is approaching. What does that mean? His words are still often unclear to me. Does he declare himself King of Israel or prophet of God and begin a new sect, or is he truly the Messiah? I am very confused, as are many of his followers.

Any thoughts or advice would be appreciated. Thank you for listening. Please pray for us.

Your fledgling student of human behavior,

Philip

Dear Kathryn, from Lazarus the resurrected.

I am sure you have heard about my incredible experience. Martha said she had written and told you how ill I was, but that is the last thing I remember. It seems everyone knows more about what happened to me than I do.

Can you imagine what it was like to wake up in a dark cave, wrapped in burial bands? Let me tell you, it was terrifying. It was hard to take a breath. I heard my name being called and recognized the voice of Jesus. I could barely walk to Jesus when he called me. Some of the townspeople unwrapped me while Martha and Mary were holding hands, jumping up and down, crying and laughing at the same time.

After I was unwrapped, my sisters kept hugging and kissing me. People just stood and watched in amazement. Jesus stood and watched for a while, letting my sisters express their ecstasy. He then came, put his hand on my shoulder, looked at me with such love, and said, "Lazarus, it is not time for you to leave this earth." It brought tears to my eyes.

Since then, nothing has been the same. Mary and Martha are hovering over me all the time and I have become a spectacle to the people of the town. I have even heard a rumor that the Pharisees are planning to do me some harm. I do not know why this is all happening to me or what I am to do with this second chance at life. I know this sounds ungrateful; I do not mean it to be. Jesus will be coming soon and I have many questions for him. I hope he has the answers.

Please pray for me.

Your friend,

Lazarus

Dear Kathryn, from Mary, the sister of Martha and Lazarus.

I am so much in love! I think of him morning, noon, and night. I close my eyes and I can see his face—those piercing dark brown eyes, his warm smile, his full, sensual lips. Each time he greets me and kisses me on the cheek, I tremble with desire.

I know he loves me, but is it as a brother loves his younger sister? My love is not sisterly. It is with all the passion, desire, and devotion that a woman can have for a man. I feel his presence, even when he is not here, and when he is here it is enough to sit at his feet and listen to his words. I would die for him if need be, and I will live for him and only him. I will do all that he asks of me. When he looks at me in that special way, I know how beautiful and special I really am. He touches my soul.

Martha gets very impatient with me and tells me to quit mooning about him. She says, "Jesus does not love you in that way and you are wasting your time," but I am content just to be in his presence. The love he talks about will have to be enough for me. While I know I am special to him, he loves everyone he meets, so I will try to practice what he preaches.

Jesus says he will not be with us for much longer. I am not sure what that means; he never explains himself. Will he have to leave the country? I wonder, because we have heard the authorities are planning to harm both him and Lazarus. If there is trouble coming, I hope I have the courage to endure and to be of use to Jesus.

Please pray for the safety of Jesus and Lazarus.

Your loving friend,

Mary

Dear Kathryn, from Sophia, who fears what the future might hold.

We have traveled many miles, crisscrossing all of Judea as Jesus has taught, preached, and worked miracles of all kinds. We have reached Bethany, our last stop before we go to Jerusalem for Passover next week. During the last year, the numbers of Jesus' supporters and believers has increased, as well as the number of those who have chosen to join the group who accompanies Jesus in his travels. This is most evident here in Bethany, after Jesus raised Lazarus from the dead.

It should be a time for celebration and joy, but there is an undercurrent causing fear and trepidation among the women. Let me try to explain what has been going on with the men in our community. Many of the women sense a growing unrest, me included. There are secret comings and goings that take place after Jesus retires for the night. The men sit around the fire until late in the night, talking in whispers until voices are raised in anger and quickly hushed. I have overheard some of those conversations and talked with the wives of some of the men. This is what I have learned.

Because of the great support of the Jewish people everywhere we go, because of the increased hardships under Roman rule, and, finally, because they firmly believe Jesus is preordained to be King of the Jews, a good number of the men believe it is time to overthrow the rule of the Romans. These same men have gone behind the back of Jesus to foment that support with enthusiasm.

For instance, it is the responsibility of Judas, James, and Andrew to enter each town we visit and watch for potential problems or dangers, to assess the safest and quickest avenue of escape if necessary. In addition to this, they have taken it upon themselves to see that a number of people with disease

137

or illness, people who need healing, are placed strategically among the cheering crowd. Their thinking is that it is also their job to ensure Jesus is seen in the best possible light—as if Jesus needed any help with this! I was not sure if Jesus was aware of any of this, so several of we women tried to raise these issues with him. He gently raised his hand in a stopping motion, saying, "Do not fear. All is well, all is well."

You know, Kathryn, when we women hear Jesus talk about peace, love, and the Kingdom of God, we hear one thing and the men hear another. We do not think of glory, riches, or power. We think of family and community, living together in loving support, where no one is excluded and all are welcome—strangers and enemies as well.

The men have another message: freedom from the yoke of the Romans, the return of the glory of Israel, with Jesus as King and they as the powerful members of his court. Almost from the beginning, the men jockeyed for position, asking Jesus, "Who is your favorite? Who will sit next to you in your Kingdom? Who will help rule?"

The hatred for the Romans is increasing as the number of Jesus' followers has increased, even though Jesus teaches us to love our enemies. I fear they think the time for a rebellion is at hand. The word is, Peter is sending a contingent of men to Jerusalem prior to our arrival to arouse the people, hoping for a great crowd to welcome him and show their support—a royal reception fit for the King of the Jews.

In the last few months, some of the men have taken to wearing swords—but not around Jesus—and there is a rumor that money has been set aside to fund the rebellion. We hear grumbling and frustration with Jesus, who they feel has no interest in their plans or their ambitions to proclaim him king. I fear they may take things into their own hands to precipitate a confrontation that would cause a violent response.

I am not alone among the women, and even some of the

more reticent men, who have these fears. The men who do not support this thinking have tried to dissuade these men, with the voices of most of the wives, mothers, and sisters echoing the path of peace—but to no avail. Jesus seems to be above the fray and, if any approach him on the subject, he repeats his answer that all will be well.

Does not someone have to put a stop to all of this plotting and inciting of hatred? We would feel the wrath not only of the Roman Legion but of the Pharisees and the Sadducees as well. Jesus' safety and life would be in danger and many Jewish lives would be lost in an ill-fated insurrection.

Please pray for a peaceful resolution to this situation with Jesus, as he always values your counsel.

Pray for everlasting peace,
Sophia

Dear Kathryn, from Martha, an overworked and underappreciated woman.

I have so much to share with you. Our lives have been in such chaos since Jesus raised my brother Lazarus from the dead. Our family has become Bethany's latest sideshow. Children peek in the windows or try to touch Lazarus if he steps out of the house. The adults stare at the three of us all the time and people are coming from other towns to also take a look at "the family." In the midst of all this, I'm trying to keep things going with going to the market, cooking, cleaning, and baking. I feel like a total wreck.

You know Lazarus was always a shy, quiet man, but he is becoming even more withdrawn. He says he remembers only being very sick and in pain, then waking up wrapped in burial bands. He was terrified. Then he heard Jesus calling his name and he waddled out of the cave. That is all he remembers, and he is tired of trying to answer all the questions.

Well, last week we got word our beloved friend Jesus was coming to visit. I cleaned the house from top to bottom, then cooked and baked all his favorite foods. I wanted everything to be perfect—and what help did I get from Mary and Lazarus? Nothing. Why do I always have to ask for their help? Can they not see what needs to be done?

Mary was mooning about the house like a lovesick puppy and Lazarus was very worried about the visit. He was looking forward to seeing his best friend, but he was afraid it would just add to the chaos and he was right. Not only was Jesus here, but many of his followers. I feared I would not have enough food or enough room for all the visitors.

Of course, I had to do all the serving. Mary just sat at the feet of Jesus, listening to his every word. Then she anointed his feet with oil and she dried them with her hair. You should have heard the uproar about the wastefulness of using expensive oil in such a manner. No one paid much attention to the food I worked so hard to prepare and I never did get to spend time with Jesus because I was so busy. What a disappointment!

Please do not mention to Jesus what I just wrote, but I knew you would understand.

Love,
Martha

Dear Kathryn, from your devoted friend Jesus.

I have just returned from Bethany and a visit with our friends Martha, Mary, and Lazarus. Martha prepared a wonderful feast for me and my friends, but she keeps herself so busy she never allows herself to just be. What a good, kind, and loving woman she is, but so afraid of seeming vulnerable and weak.

Well, she cannot hide who she is from me. I had to go to the kitchen to seek her out or we would never have had a chance to talk. She kept herself so busy with serving and cleaning up, it was difficult to approach her. I told her how much I loved her, how much I appreciated her. I am not sure she heard me, but I will keep telling her until she gets the message.

Poor Lazarus is in much distress, so unsure of his place in the world, his role, his future. It is all so simple—it is the same for Lazarus as for all people—but they seem not to hear or understand. Just love one another. I think he felt better after we talked. I also told him to be careful because of the rumors of danger.

And then there is Mary. Mary is a woman who loves with every cell in her body, who accepts the gift of the moment, not demanding or desiring more. How blessed is she! She will help Lazarus and Martha to learn to love openly and unconditionally. She reminds me of another Mary, my mother, Mary.

I am worried about my mother. If something should happen to me, she will suffer much. Her torment will be worse in the watching than mine in the enduring of the experience. While it is not something I am looking forward to, this last act of life is preordained. I am not sure where, when, or exactly what is to occur, but it will happen soon.

So, please do me a favor: Spend some time with my mother.

She will need all the love and support of our friends during the troubled days ahead. You, being a mother, will know what she is going through.

I have my own fears about what lies ahead. What if I cannot be the son my Father wants me to be? What if I lose faith, lose courage? My apostles do not understand what is to happen, so it feels so lonely.

Kathryn, you are a help to many people. Thank you for listening.

Your loving friend,

Jesus

Dear Kathryn, from Jesus, your devoted friend and brother.

Thank you so much for your loving message. I know you wrote at the behest of some of my women followers. They are a devoted, loyal, and passionate group. I know they have many fears about the future and my safety. I have reassured them that all is in the hands of my Father, but it is not a concept easily grasped by them, as well as my disciples.

When I first met the people that follow and live with me now, they were like little children seeking a parent who would make all their individual dreams and hopes come true, a parent who would protect and save them from the realities of their lives. They wanted a savior, a Messiah.

They have learned much since that time, but now are of an age where they think they know best. They have listened to my words for three years, but have not come to understand the message. They hear what they want to hear, see what they want to see. Reality for them is not the reality of the Father, but of their own imperfect humanness.

My time is short and they sense something is going to happen, even though what they want to see happen will not come to pass. I love them and, even though I will be gone, I will not abandon them. It is only after I am gone that the scales will fall from their eyes and they will understand the message of my words.

You are truly a woman of God and the work you do is God's work.

Your devoted friend and brother,

Jesus

Dear Kathryn, from Andrew, a concerned servant of Jesus.

We have just completed a triumphal march into Jerusalem. Hundreds of people lined the streets, laying palm branches and their cloaks on the road before the donkey Jesus was riding, while shouting, "Blessed is he who comes in the name of the Lord!" The other disciples and I walked behind Jesus during the whole time and marveled at the happenings. We were watching closely because we feared the donkey would stumble on all that debris on the road and Jesus would be injured.

As the donkey picked his way through all the branches and cloaks on the road, Jesus raised his hand many times in blessing over the people. He moved his head slowly from side to side, attempting to make eye contact with each person.

We were all stunned by the reception he was receiving. Here we were in Jerusalem, Jesus being hailed as Prophet, King of the Jews, Messiah, or Savior of the nation, when just a few days ago we had to spirit him away from a town where the leaders had attempted to incite people to harm him. This was not the first time that kind of thing had happened either; it is happening more and more frequently. Jesus is making powerful enemies.

I do not know what to think. Judas, who is a master at protecting Jesus, has a sixth sense in anticipating potential danger to Jesus. He is scrupulous in planning his entry and exit routes from each town, advises on who can or cannot be trusted, sees that several of us are always with him, and feels he can protect Jesus under any and all circumstances. He also feels the time is now for the rebellion and Jesus should declare his kingship.

Peter, on the other hand, feels Jesus should slow down, let things settle a bit, and take some time away from Jerusalem, so as not to give the authorities more reason to feel threatened by his teachings. They feel a loss of power as people turn to Jesus and that will make them even more dangerous. I do not know what to think as this turmoil swirls about Jesus. He seems at peace, and resigned, constantly reminding us to place our trust in Yahweh.

Please pray for Jesus' continued safety.

Your friend,

Andrew

Dear Kathryn, from Judas, the forlorn.

By the time you get this letter I will have taken my life. I wanted someone to understand why and what I did to bring myself to this moment. I am on the Mount of Olives, the site of my so-called betrayal. Kathryn, I would not have betrayed the man I loved most in the whole world.

As I sit here, I can remember vividly the first time I met Jesus, three years ago. I had heard of the new rabbi and his preaching, but had decided not to go see him—I was too busy. But he sought me out, coming to my home, looking at me with those piercing eyes, full of love and compassion, and saying, "Judas, come, follow me"—and I did.

I knew the time of Israel's deliverance from Rome was at hand. Jesus must be the Messiah, the one to lead the revolution and become King of the Jews. I felt so blessed and honored to be part of it all. He was the answer to my prayers. But, you know, Jesus is not a practical man. I was the keeper of the purse and, if I had not put money aside to arm the people when the time came to rebel, he would have given it all to the poor.

As we traveled together, he gained more and more followers, as well as the attention of the authorities. We often had to plan how to avoid his arrest and keep him safe. We often used diversionary tactics to slip him out of town, out of the grasp of those who sought to harm him. We would secrete him in the home of his loyal followers. Protecting Jesus was one of my primary responsibilities and I was very good at it. I loved him very much.

And yet, with so many devoted followers proclaiming him the Messiah, King of the Jews, he was still not ready to begin the revolution. So, a thought occurred to me: Maybe I could create a situation that would be the catalyst to begin the uprising.

I knew in my heart that the people would never allow any

harm to come to Jesus. So, I met with the Pharisees, leading them to believe I was disillusioned with Jesus and needed some money for a new start. We planned where and how they would apprehend Jesus. At the Seder meal, he announced, "Someone will betray me," letting me know he knew of the plan and supported it.

Kathryn, he never told me to stop. What else was I to think? Our time was here! Jesus would call upon the people to rescue him. The overthrow of the Romans would begin.

But everything went wrong. Jesus did not call for rescue. In fact, he chastised Peter for coming to his defense and cutting off the ear of one of the guards. The Pharisees paid scores of people to stand in the crowd and scream for his execution as he appeared before Pilate. I went to the authorities to return the money and begged for his life, but they just laughed and threw me out.

So, as I sit here in the Mount of Olives, they are torturing Jesus and preparing him for crucifixion. I cannot tolerate the humiliation, the pain, the shame. To know I am responsible for the death of my dearest, most beloved friend is more than I can bear.

I should have waited until he said the time was right. I loved him so much. I would have fought at his side and died to protect him if need be. I would have done whatever he commanded. But, instead of being an advisor and confidante of the King of Israel, I will be forever known as the betrayer of Jesus the Christ.

This I cannot endure. I have committed an unforgivable sin. I shall die here in the garden where, just a few hours ago, I kissed Jesus on the lips to begin this horror.

Remember me with not so much bitterness,

Judas Iscariot

Jesus' Death and Resurrection

Dear Kathryn, from Malchus, servant to the High Priest Caiaphas.

You do not know me, but I was with my master the night Jesus the Nazarene was arrested. I feel compelled to write and tell you about some of the incredible events that took place during and after that arrest.

Two days before the arrest, a man called Judas came to the Temple and asked to speak to the Council. I escorted him to their chambers and was ordered to leave the area. I was unable to hear what was said, but, after Judas left, I could hear arguing going on among the priests. I thought no more of it until last night, when a detachment of soldiers, Temple police, and priests gathered. Something big was going to happen, but we slaves did not know what it was, just that each of us was to accompany our master.

The entire cadre of men and their slaves headed out toward Gethsemane. As we approached the garden, the men quieted down and the armed contingent drew their swords. I still had no idea what was happening.

We quietly entered the garden and headed toward a group of men who were seated around one man, who seemed to be speaking to them. They all stood quickly as they heard us approaching, surrounding the man who was still in the middle of the circle. The soldiers surrounded the circle of men, who turned to face the soldiers, and the few in the circle who were armed drew their swords. No one spoke, but it was very tense and I felt a bloody fight would erupt at any moment. I then recognized the man in the center of the circle: It was the Rabbi Jesus. He was the only one who seemed calm and unafraid.

Jesus gently made his way through both of the circles to meet Judas who moved forward toward him. I still had no idea what was happening. Judas greeted Jesus with a kiss. The

Temple police then stepped forward to restrain Jesus. One of his men rushed forward, waving his sword, and severed my ear.

For a moment I felt nothing, and I heard a shout, "Hold!" Then excruciating pain dropped me to my knees. Blood spewed into my eyes and down my neck. My ear hung loose from my head, and I automatically pressed my hand over my ear to hold it in place. I could barely see, as my face was covered in blood.

Someone put his arm around my back and said, in my good ear, "Do not be afraid." I looked up and saw that it was Jesus. He put one hand over my hand that was holding my severed ear and his other hand on my right temple, exerting gentle pressure toward the injured side. I am not sure how long he held my head, but, during that time, I felt a strange sensation run through my whole body, finally gathering at my injured ear. "You are healed," Jesus said.

He then removed his hands, helped me to my feet, and used the hem of his robe to wipe the blood from my face and neck. I touched my ear and it was healed, as if it had never been injured. Jesus stood looking at me with such tenderness, but he never said another word. Then he turned and went willingly with those who came to arrest him. When I looked around, the men who had been with him were nowhere to be seen.

As I was in a state of shock, several of the other slaves helped me back to our quarters and I immediately fell into a deep sleep. When I woke after several hours, my thoughts turned to the happenings of the night. I remember little; things were a blur. Who is this man who has the power to heal? I decided to find out what had happened to Jesus.

I learned he was being held in prison, here in Jerusalem. I felt a deep need to see him and talk to him. I had so many questions. I told the guard at the prison, whom I knew, that Caiaphas had sent me, so he allowed me to enter the cell. Jesus was lying on a mat and clearly was in pain as he pushed himself up to a seated position. His face was swollen, one eye almost closed, and his hair matted with blood from what must have been a scalp wound. He smiled when he recognized me, and I saw two teeth were missing.

I sat in front of him and he asked me about my ear. I said it was fine, then asked how he felt. He said, "All is in the hands of the Father." I asked him why he had healed me when the group I was with meant to do him harm. He smiled again, then he told me many things. He said that, though I am a slave, I am truly a free man in his Father's eyes. I am loved and honored as God's beloved son and that makes us brothers. He knew things about me and my past that no one could know and said that more than my ear had been healed. He said, as time goes by, I will experience many changes in the way I think, feel, and behave. I believed him with every fiber in my body. How could I doubt such a man?

He asked if I would do him a service. He wanted to write a letter to you and asked if I would have it delivered. I humbly agreed. I went to gather pen and paper and waited outside the cell as he wrote. You will find his letter enclosed with mine.

The next day, Jesus was crucified and died. I do not understand why a man such as he had to suffer and die, but I plan to learn more about him, and count myself as one of his followers. My faith grows, despite his death.

I am sure we will meet in the future, as I count you and his disciples as family.

Sincerely,

Malchus

Dear Kathryn, from Jesus, the forsaken.

In the past, you have been a stalwart friend and supporter, both for me and my family. Tonight I need such comfort and support. As I write this letter, it feels as if you are sitting here with me in my cell.

I was arrested in Gethsemane a few hours ago and brought to the house of the High Priest, where I await judgment in the morning, when I will be taken to the Sanhedrin. I sit here feeling abandoned and terrified about what will happen tomorrow.

After the Passover meal, my apostles and I gathered in Gethsemane to pray, for I knew I was to be sorely tested and I was terrified about what was to come. In my anguish, I cried out to my Father, "Let this cup pass!" then lost consciousness and convulsed, for when I awoke, I had lost all my bodily fluids and was sobbing and crying out for my Father to help me. Shortly after that, the priests, elders, and soldiers arrived, surrounded my disciples, and I was arrested. Peter jumped to my defense and cut off the ear of a slave of one of the priests. I called for all violence to stop, my friends ran away, and I healed the man's ear.

On the way to the High Priest's house, the mocking, beatings, and insults began. It was so humiliating. I became angry. I wanted to call on the angels of the Lord to rain terror on my torturers, but I just kept praying, "Your will, not mine, be done." So, here I sit, alone in this room, wondering if I can face more of this tomorrow.

I am in physical pain, but the emotional pain is much worse. I am feeling alone, abandoned, confused, and doubting my courage. The slave, Malchus, has come to thank me for healing his ear. We have spoken of many things. I told him of my Father's love and we were both comforted. He is a gift from Yahweh to sustain me through the night, as is this letter.

Kathryn, you remember the doubt and confusion I felt as I began my ministry, years ago—desperately trying to do the will of Yahweh, never quite sure which path was the right one, until I realized I did not need to know. I was being used for a higher purpose, which never was completely revealed to me. I was the tool and Yahweh the carpenter. I am reminded of that tonight, and my greatest fear is that I will fail in my task and disappoint my father. What if I behave in cowardly way, beg for mercy, denounce my father? Is it possible? It is not so much that I fear death, for I will return to my father, but the process of dying itself.

I am fatigued, but feel a sense of relief and calmness for the writing of this letter, along with the visit from Malchus, both of which give me the courage to face my fears. I thank you for being my friend.

Pray with me that I do as the Father has asked of me.

Love,
Jesus

Dear Kathryn, from Philip, a terrified disciple of Jesus.

It has been chaos since Jesus was arrested on the Mount of Olives last night. After one feeble attempt at protecting Jesus, we, his disciples, ran and scattered as if being pursued by the devil himself. Someone shouted out, "Gather at the place where we had our Passover meal!"

No one seemed to be giving chase, so, after a while, I stopped to catch my breath. "Oh God in heaven," I prayed, "What is happening? What will happen to Jesus? What should I do?" I decided to head back to the Mount, hiding in the shadows whenever possible. I was still terrified that soldiers were looking for us. When someone noticed me and spoke to me, I feigned deafness.

There were many people about, since it was the end of Passover. The closer I got to the Mount of Olives, there were small groups of people gathered, speaking about what had just occurred, so I stopped to listen. People were agitated and angry, trying to get answers from anyone who said they were in the garden at the time. There was yelling, and disputes about what actually happened, and even pushing and shoving. I was on the edge of one group and asked the person next to me what was going on.

"The Rabbi Jesus was arrested by the Temple guards," he said, "and there was a great fight and he was taken away." He did not know if Jesus was hurt, but many had been injured. "How could this have come to pass? He was such a holy man," he said as I was walking away.

I headed slowly to the upper room, not wanting to call attention to myself as one of Jesus' followers. I walked by the house of Caiaphas. The courtyard was filled with guards, as well as other people. I was afraid to go in, as I might be recognized. For a minute, I thought I saw Peter, but I was not sure. As I continued on my way to the meeting place, I met up with some of the other followers and by the time we got to the room, other disciples were there who had heard about the incident and had gathered as well.

We sat, whispering or in silence. You could smell the stench of the fear in the room. We waited for our leaders to arrive. After a while, we started to get restless and the accusations and blaming began. Whose job was it to protect Jesus? Did anyone know or suspect what Judas was planning? Were there others of us involved in the plot? Why were not more of us armed?

Where was Peter? No one knew. Where was John? Someone said he went to tell Mary what had happened. Men were no longer silent. There was much breast-beating, outbursts of repentance, and name-calling.

Kathryn, I sat in one corner of the room, feeling shame so deep I cannot describe it. I do not know how long we were there before Peter finally arrived. His face was ashen, his eyes glazed, and he was dirty and disheveled. By the time he arrived, there were thirty or so disciples present, with only Judas and John absent.

We waited for Peter to speak. He was silent for what seemed to be a long time, then someone shouted, "Let us arm ourselves and free Jesus!" but we were a room full of cowards who would not risk their lives, even for the man who meant so much to us. Andrew went over to Peter, pulled him to the center of the room, took him by the shoulder, and shook him. Nothing—no response from him.

What happened in those few minutes in the garden? We lost all courage, all our hopes and dreams. Jesus was the Messiah. He was to be the King of Israel. How had we let this happen? Who is at fault? Was Jesus deceiving us when he said, "I confer my kingdom on you, that you may eat and drink at my table in my kingdom, and you will sit on thrones judging the twelve tribes of Israel"?

Mary Magdalene and Lydia, the sister of Matthew, suddenly rushed into the room. Mary was livid. Her face was red with anger, her eyes spitting fire. Shame and silence filled the room as she screamed, "How could you let this happen?!" No one responded. She looked at us with disgust and started giving orders. "Bartholomew, find Joseph of Arimathea and see if he can help. I have sent one of the women to the Romans to see if Jesus can have visitors. If so, I will go to him and find out what he wants us to do. John is staying and tending to his mother. Andrew, you and Thomas go out and see if you can find Judas, but be careful—we do not want the Pharisees to arrest anyone else, as they are probably searching for us. Try and talk to others who are sympathetic to our cause. See if you can find out any more information about what is happening."

Like a whirlwind, she continued: "James, John, you will be responsible for gathering food, water, and blankets, for we do not know how long we will be hiding in this room. I have spoken to the landlord. He supports us and agrees to this plan and will provide us with a second room if necessary. All of you who are leaving, be on the watch for other disciples and friends and direct them here. Tell no one else where we are."

She clapped her hands and said, "Now, go and be careful. We should have more information by morning. The rest of you, stay here and think on what wretched men you are." With that concluding statement, she left. Still no movement or words from Peter.

We are so desperate and in need of your prayers and intercession with Yahweh. I will ask the landlord to get this letter to you tonight.

Philip

Dear Kathryn, from a devastated Mary Magdalene.

Yesterday, the Romans crucified Jesus and I lost forever the man who loved me as no other had. From the first moment he looked into my eyes and touched my hand, I became a different woman. He loved me, passionately and unconditionally. He made me feel valued, loved, respected, beautiful, desirable, intelligent, capable, happy, excited, and peaceful. I could go on and on, but I know you understand. You know the whole story of where and how he found me.

We spent so much time together. Jesus needed me as much as I needed him. I listened to his fears, his hopes, his frustrations. I held him as he wept in discouragement. I could sense how he felt and what he needed. We enjoyed the important things together: a sunset, the sound of music, the face of a child.

He often held me, both of us trembling with desire, and he would tell me how much I meant to him—too much to have a physical relationship. He wanted me to know how valuable I was to him—as a human being, not just as a woman. Time and time again, he would say, "Mary, never let anyone use you again.... Another will come into your life who will take you even further in your journey of healing and wholeness."

"I do not want another, I want you," I would say—and now he is dead. I will never see him again, feel his touch, hear his voice. How will I live without him? I have an emptiness in my whole being. It is like the winds of the desert have swept away all the life force in my body, leaving a dry, dead corpse.

And yet I have such an anger. I am angry at the Romans, angry at the Pharisees, and especially angry at his so-called friends, those twelve disciples that were with him that night. They all deserted him. they were such cowards! They are, at this moment, hiding in the rooms where they had the Seder meal with him, fearful the same fate might befall them.

And now, all they talk about is their disappointment that Jesus was not the Messiah. I did not follow him because he was the Messiah! I loved and followed him because he was Jesus, the kindest, most generous, honest, loving, sensitive, bravest, most intelligent man I had ever met. And, if you ask any of the other women, I am sure they would say the same thing. But the men—they wanted power, prestige, the Kingdom of Israel restored, and they thought Jesus was a means to that end. That is what they are grieving. They lost the chance to be among the followers of the Messiah, the Ruler of Israel, while I lost my reason for being. I lost the man who breathed life, love, and forgiveness into my soul, who was in my every thought. Our energies had become as one.

Why, God, why did you allow this to happen? What kind of God are you? I wished I had the courage to end my pain, but I too am a coward—too cowardly to end my life and too much of a coward to face my life without Jesus.

Kathryn, what am I to do? What am I to do? Please, please help me.

Mary Magdalene

Dear Kathryn, from Miriam the traumatized.

I have been witness to a most horrifying experience and I need to share it with someone who will understand. You remember the young rabbi, Jesus of Nazareth? Our people had him crucified yesterday and I was there.

I had seen one crucifixion before and I promised myself I would never, ever attend another again. But, when the news reached the neighborhood about what was happening, I was drawn by a force I cannot describe.

First of all, I was in denial. It could not be Jesus they were executing—the kind, loving, empathetic healer. The teacher who shared his wisdom with us. The one who spoke of loving one another, taking care of one another, and teaching us to look deeply into our hearts and do away with pride, prejudice, hatred. and anger. The man who cured the sick and lame, who treated sinners and saints alike, whose eyes pierced the marrow of my bones and who changed my life forever. I loved him very much.

When I reached the praetorium, they had already scourged him and hammered a crown of thorns upon his head. Blood was dripping down his face and into his eyes. His back was ripped open by the slash of the whip. They placed a purple cloak around him and began to mock him, yelling out, "Hail, King of the Jews!" There were tears in his eyes, and I could not believe it, but he looked at the soldiers with tenderness and love. What kind of man is this?

Then they began the trip to Golgotha. He was made to carry his own crossbeam, although this was not always the case. The beam was much too heavy for him, especially in his weakened condition. The soldiers pulled a man from the crowd, a foreigner, to help him carry it.

I was dizzy from the heat and my vision was blurred from my tears. I found myself repeating, "This cannot be happening," over and over, like a mantra. I joined a group of women who walked beside him, who were praying aloud and asking the angels to rescue him. The air was filled with the pain emanating from Jesus, the pain from those who loved him, and especially from his mother.

Mary walked slowly and erect, never taking her eyes from the face of her son. She did not look where she walked; the crowd just made way for her. There was not one tear in her eye, even though her face was a picture of pure agony. She did not emit a sound or shed a tear, as if to spare her son any additional pain. I have never seen anything like it.

The pain I felt in my chest kept rising to my throat and I fought to control it. Then a woman next to me let out a moan. It broke the dam that had been holding back all the pain we were suffering. Women began wailing, crying out to Yahweh, rocking and holding themselves, reaching out, trying to touch Jesus for one last time. Everyone lost control, except Mary. She continued her last walk with her son, with a quiet, steady march, as if she were the one going to her death. Jesus looked at us, stopped for a moment, and said, "Women of Jerusalem, do not cry for me, but cry for your children." For generations to come, I fear our people will be held accountable for this horrific act.

When the soldiers placed Jesus on the cross and began pounding the nails into his hands and feet, there was a moan that passed through the crowd with each blow. Mary's body jerked, as if she were experiencing the pain each time the hammer struck the head of the nail. Jesus let out a low, guttural moan, almost animal-like. It was terrible.

Then the wait began. We were all hoping it would not be prolonged, because of the agony he was enduring, and we were very grateful it only went on for three hours. For the entire time, Mary stood beneath the cross, transfixed. Her eyes never left her son. She spoke to no one, refused food or drink. Jesus spoke several times, but I could not hear what he said. I saw Mary and

John nod their heads in response to something he said. John was the only one of his disciples there at the foot of the cross.

Many women who followed him stood with him that day in his suffering. Among us were Mary's sister Martha, Mary Magdalene, Joanna, and several women whom I did not know. Jesus' head hung so low on his chest you could not see his face. Then, finally, he said, so clearly we all heard him, "It is done." Then he died. Mary collapsed at the foot of the cross, and sounds of grief filled the air with such magnitude there was almost no room for air to breathe. John and Martha tended to Mary, and she finally took a drink of water.

When they finally took Jesus down from the cross, Mary was sitting on the ground. They placed his body in her arms. she held him tightly, his head resting against her shoulder, his body across her lap. She began rocking and singing to him, one of those simple songs we all sing to our children when they are little. She finally held his head in the crook of her arm so she could look into his face. She used her sleeve to wipe away the blood, sweat, and dirt. She stroked back his hair. She covered his private parts with her headscarf. Then she began to kiss him, first on the forehead, then each eye, each check, and lastly on his lips. This was all done with love, devotion, and the deepest of reverence. She stroked his hair, his arms, and held a handkerchief over the wound in his side. She spoke to him quietly of her love for him, how much joy he had brought to her, how proud she had been to call him son, and how much she would miss him.

This went on for quite a while, with no one interfering. Then she suddenly looked up and seemed to become aware of us. She made eye contact with me and nodded, giving me and the others permission to approach the two of them. She continued to hold him while, one at a time, people spoke to him, held or kissed his hand, stroked his hair, kissed his feet, or just laid their hands on his body.

Then it was time to prepare him for burial. Simon and Joseph of Arimathea arrived and gently removed Jesus from his mother's arms. They wrapped him in a linen cloth and, as they lifted him to carry him away, Mary stood, her arms raised to the heavens, and screamed the name of Jesus with such agony and force, I shall hear it the rest of my life. Then she collapsed.

I could not bear any more. There were many present to attend to Mary and I needed to escape the scene. I felt a tremendous need to reach the safety of my home and embrace my children. The day will be embedded in my mind for the rest of my life. There seemed to be no sense to it all. I pray for relief from the pain and for peace and understanding, but I am sure it will be a long time coming, if it ever does.

Pray for all of us, especially for his mother Mary.

Love,

Miriam

Dear Kathryn, from Veronica, devoted follower of the Rabbi Jesus.

I have been blessed with such a magnificent gift. I have in my possession my mantle—with the face of Jesus on it!

Let me tell you what happened. The horrible day of his execution was very hot—not a cloud in the sky and the sun's rays felt like fire as it struck bare skin. Jesus was weak from being scourged earlier, from the crown of the thorns hammered into his head, from the weight of the crossbeam, and from having nothing to eat or drink since the night before.

There was a crowd, expressing very mixed feelings about this execution. Many people stood on the sidelines, or followed him as he moved toward the crucifixion site. Some men were jeering at him, vendors were selling sweets and fruits, but many of the women, who had followed him for years, were wailing in distress for the loss of their Lord. The whole atmosphere had the feeling of some macabre entertainment the Romans had staged for the locals.

As Jesus approached the area where I was standing, I was able to get a good look at him. his back was covered with strips of raw flesh, hanging loose from the muscle. His face was covered with sweat and his blood oozed from the wounds in his head. He kept blinking his eyes to clear them, so he could see where he was going.

He stumbled and fell, right in front of me, and I could no longer stand to see him in such pain and humiliation. I rushed forward, tearing the mantle from my head. I knelt and gently wiped his face. I was out of control with my grief, sobbing so hard I could not speak. He looked at me with those eyes of his and said, "Veronica, do not forget the poor." One of the soldiers grabbed me and pushed me back into the crowd, while another struck Jesus, telling him to get up.

I was so upset! It was my last opportunity to speak to my beloved Jesus, and all I could do was cry. I could not continue to the execution. Instead, I wrapped my mantle around me and sought the solace of my home.

Once I got home, I collapsed and lay sobbing, asking myself what Jesus was requesting of me when he said, "remember the poor." I have often provided for women and children whom he sent to my home, which is also my weaving shop. It is small, but I have been able to provide for myself and the children since Ephraim died, though it has been very difficult. The Romans have increased the amount of taxes all of us are required to pay. Many of our people have lost businesses or homes to these unjust taxes. People no longer have the means to help each other. In fact, hard feelings and feuds have developed among families and between neighbors because of so much need.

Jesus would send women and children to me who had no others to help them. I would feed and clothe them, often putting these women to work in my shop. We have woven cloth for Jesus and his followers from the beginning of his ministry. In fact, the day he died, he was wearing some of our clothing. He used to say, "Veronica's weaving is so beautiful, beyond description!" Often, I would worry that there would not be enough food to go around, but, by some miracle, there was always enough. "I have remembered the poor. What more does he want from me?" I thought. "I can do no more."

When I rose from weeping and picked up my mantle from the floor, there was the imprint of the face of Jesus, exactly as he looked in the moment that I wiped his face. I gasped. Who was I to receive this miracle? Was this his way of telling me that I can always do more? Does this mean my job is to take care of those who have no resources of their own?

At that moment, I knew that I had nothing to worry about. Yahweh would provide, and I would dedicate my life to the purpose that Jesus had asked of me the day he died. I will be showing the mantle to his other followers when it is safe to meet again. I hope you have a chance to see it as well.

Love,

Veronica

Dear Kathryn, from Mary, the grief-stricken mother of Jesus.

I can barely write these words or think these thoughts: I have lost my beloved son, Jesus. I cannot eat, I cannot sleep, I feel a pain in my heart so intense it makes it difficult to breathe. I lie in bed, asking God to take me too.

Jesus tried to prepare me, but I never understood completely. He told me many times he was about his father's business. He said there would be times of great sorrow in our lives, but never in my wildest dreams did I imagine he would die such a horrible death as crucifixion.

What I did know, from the moment he was conceived, is that he was a gift from God. When I held him in my arms for the first time, I wept for joy. I was in awe of this miracle and the depth of my feelings as he suckled at my breast—this beautiful and special infant.

Those feelings became more intense as he grew. When he followed me as a toddler everywhere I went, asking question after question. He grew strong as a young boy, working at Joseph's side, learning to be a carpenter. He was so anxious to please his father and make us both proud. He was pious young man. He studied, learned our history, and he taught and loved all whom he met. He was my beloved son—and now he is gone.

All those years I protected him. I kept him safe from harm, made sure he had enough to eat, tended his wounds, held him when he was hurt or frightened, woke in the night to hear him cry out in his sleep and reassured him all was well. When he had pain, I felt pain. When he was happy, I was happy. I would have died for him, bore any pain for him, and probably would have killed to protect him.

He was my son, and now he is gone. I will never see him again, hear his voice, feel his touch or kiss his face. How will I survive?

Witnessing his torture was unbearable. I prayed for his death, to relieve him of the suffering, but when death came, I said, "No, no! Do not take my son from me!" First Joseph, and now Jesus. How much is a woman to bear? Yesterday, we put him in a tomb and when they rolled the stone in place it felt like the stone was placed in my heart.

Thank you for hearing me, Kathryn. I know you understand. His friends here in Jerusalem look to me for support and hope. I have none to give. John has been very good to me, but I had to talk to you—another mother, a mother who I hope never has to endure the unbearable pain of losing a child.

May God continue to bless and protect your children.

Love,

Mary

Dear Kathryn, from Peter, the coward.

What an ordeal we have been through. We lost our brother Jesus, our savior, our last hope for restoring the nation of Israel. What must he have been thinking, when he asked me, three years ago, to leave all to join him? He even came to depend on me, asking me to lead in his absence, telling me I was to be the rock upon which he would build his faith community. Some rock I turned out to be—me, Simon, who is such a braggart, who swore I would be at his side forever, who then not only deserted him in his hour of need, I even lied, refusing to admit I even knew him—not once, but three times. I was willing to let him face his death alone to save my worthless skin.

If only I could control what I say! The thought comes into my head and directly out my mouth. "Of course, Lord, I will be there for you." "Certainly, Lord, if you must wash my feet, I want you to wash my whole body." "Yes, Lord, I will stay awake and pray with you." "Yes, Lord, I will give my life for you!"

But did I do any of these things? NO! I was grandiose, I was proud. I was a favorite of Jesus, the Messiah. Oh, how I have failed him. I am such a coward!

He has only been gone two days and oh, how I miss him! Oh, how I wish things had been different! I wish I could have been the man he thought I was. I wish I would have been courageous and loyal. Will I ever forgive myself? I do not think so. It is something I will have to live with the rest of my life. Will the pain of his absence and my cowardice ever leave? I do not think so.

Everyone is looking to me for direction and I have none to give. We at least have each other, those that loved him so intensely. Hopefully we can support each other in the difficult days ahead. I have no idea what is to become of us. We have the women to think about and care for. And yet, they were the courageous and steadfast ones. Not one deserted him. They remained with him, even to the foot of the cross. Maybe we should look to them for direction and guidance.

I am in need of much prayer if I am to survive. I am looking to you for those prayers.

Humbly,
Simon Peter

Dear Kathryn, from the revolutionary patriot of Israel, Barabbas.

You will not believe what those fools in Jerusalem did last week. You know I have been fighting the Romans for the past twenty years. I hate them with every fiber of my body. I have done all in my power to bring down that evil, corrupt government. They have stolen our country and our homes, raped our women, and murdered our children. I have stolen from them, killed them whenever possible, urged all to rebel, and have even killed Jews who have collaborated with the enemy.

Last week, the day before Sabbath, I was being held by the Romans, awaiting execution. Late that night, they arrested the holy man, Jesus the Nazorean. The next morning, we could hear the crowd calling for his death, screaming over and over, "Crucify him, crucify him!" There were already three of us condemned to die that day, and it looked like Jesus was going to be the fourth.

A guard came to the cell, yelling, "Barabbas, step forward!" I had no idea what was happening. I was taken to the praetorium, where Pilate and Jesus stood facing the angry crowd. Standing in front of this mob were the High Priests, leading the shout for death.

Then—this is where it becomes unbelievable—Pilate asked the crowd, "Who should I release, Barabbas or Jesus?" The crowd yelled "Barabbas!" over and over.

I could not understand what was happening. I had heard this man teach—he spoke of peace, love, kindness, and caring, never a harsh word, except for the time he threw the moneychangers out of the Temple. Now, they wanted to take his life and save mine!

I tried to speak, but one of the guards put the scarf from his armor over my mouth. How could I let this man give his life in my place? I was ready to die, and my chance to be a martyr for the cause was being taken away!

And so it happened. They released me and Jesus was crucified later that day. I watched for a while, but thought it was no longer safe, so I headed for the hills of Samaria, which is where I am as I write you this letter.

These events are beyond my understanding and I need time to ponder these happenings and what they all mean.

Israel's devoted servant,

Barabbas

Dear Kathryn, from Marcus Aurelias, former Centurion in the Army of Rome.

I was a centurion and commander of a cohort assigned to the Praetorium in Jerusalem. My men and I were part of the group who arrested the Rabbi Jesus the night of the Passover festival. Earlier that day, the Jewish council requested our assistance in arresting a disrupter of the peace and an enemy of Rome. They gave me no name. We were to gather after sunset at the house of Caiaphas, the High Priest.

How I hated to be involved in these petty Jewish political arguments. We were the last to arrive at the house. Already there were the Temple police, many men from the council, and their slaves to serve their masters and carry torches to light the way. There was no moon and it was very dark.

I was told the criminal would be found in the garden at Gethsemane. My men and I led the way. It seemed an easy task, one man against so many, what could be a problem? Everyone quieted as we approached the garden. I saw ten or twelve men, seated around a person in the middle. A few men were standing, leaning against trees. All seemed to be listening intently. As soon as I saw the number of men, I signaled my men to draw their weapons. This could go badly if we were not careful. I wished no violence. This was supposed to be a simple arrest.

A man came forth from our group and started toward the man in the middle and I thought, "Now what?" Fortunately, the crowd seemed to know him and let him through. He walked right up to the man in the middle and greeted him with a kiss. As if this was a signal of some sort, the Temple police moved forward to arrest him.

As it became clear what was happening, the men in the garden jumped to a fighting stance, some drawing weapons. They kept the man who was speaking in the middle of their

173

protective circle. It appeared they had no concern for their own safety. They seemed unaware that they were outnumbered and facing a trained fighting force of the Roman Empire. They were ready to protect whoever stood in their midst. The Jewish contingent dropped back at the first sign of violence, pushing their slaves in front of them, and I thought, "This is not turning out as I expected."

I ordered my men to encircle the group double-time. Suddenly a man rushed forward, brandishing his sword, and attacked one of the slaves. Blood began pouring from the side of his head. My men reacted immediately and began to engage the enemy. Suddenly, a voice shouted "Hold!" with such authority that everyone stopped, as if frozen, including my men.

I heard someone say, "His ear has been cut off." The man who had been in the middle of the circle rushed through the lines to the wounded man and held his head with both hands. I recognized him—it was the Rabbi Jesus. We all stood there, stunned, as he prayed over the wounded man. The bleeding stopped, and Jesus helped the man to stand. His ear looked fine to me. It must have been a scalp wound—you know how they bleed.

Jesus then turned toward the Temple police and surrendered.

All of this happened so quickly—it could not have taken more than two or three minutes. We all breathed a sigh of relief, for it could have been a night with injuries or even deaths. While all this was happening, the other men had disappeared into the night.

We followed the Temple police as they brought Jesus to the High Priest Caiaphas for questioning. My men and I waited in the courtyard. It was very cold and we sat around the fire, trying to keep warm, drinking wine and trying to make sense of what had just happened. More than one soldier swore the man's ear was hanging by a thread before the Rabbi healed him.

The courtyard was crowded with people, who always flock

to where there has been trouble. They were shouting at each other, accusing one another of being in league with Jesus. I wonder—in league with what? I had seen and heard Jesus preach many times, since it was my job to keep the peace and prevent insurrection. I never heard him speak in anger or in rebellion. In fact, he spoke of loving your enemy. When I heard what the people were saying, I laughed out loud, because these accusations were without any merit. In fact, they were as far from the truth as possible.

I did hear about miracle cures, but the Jews are such a hysterical race, so who could believe their stories? That is, I had felt that way until my friend Tyrus Sextus, commander of the Capernaum area, wrote and told me of a miracle he himself had witnessed.

It seems a beloved slave in his household was sick unto death, so my friend sought out Jesus to cure his slave. Tyrus said Jesus had not needed even to enter his house to see the slave. He just said, "It will be done." When Tyrus returned to his house, the slave was out of bed, performing his household duties. He had been cured. My friend is an honorable man and does not lie. But I did not know what to believe. I thought he might have been in the hinterlands too long. It certainly did not appear to me that Jesus was a danger to Rome, but the Sanhedrin must feel threatened by such preaching and healing stories.

The Temple guards brought Jesus out and said they were through with him. Handing him off to my men, they told me, "Lock him up." It looked like the police had beaten him about the face. There was much muttering among my men. We all resented fetching and carrying for the Jews.

I had my men take Jesus to the prison and place him in a cell with orders that we were to refrain from any kind of abuse. Later that night, I went to the cell to make sure he would live until morning. The words he spoke to me that night have changed my life. He held no bitterness or rancor toward me or my men.

175

He said, "I have come for just as you. You are my brother and I forgive you, as my Father forgives you." He told me many things about myself that no one could know. He spoke of my friend's great faith and how I had doubted his word about this healed slave. He said, since I am a leader of men, I have the ability to change the world, to let my faith lead me.

I saw that he had food and water. I told him I did not know what was to happen in the morning and I had no authority to intervene. He knew this and said, "All that is happening is ordained." This man, a devout Jew, was not a threat to Rome, but the Jewish leaders were fearful of losing their power. Everything I believed in was shaken that night.

It has been several weeks since his death and there have been many changes in my life. I remember every word Jesus said to me and have written the words in my journal to share with others. I remember the sound of his voice, the look in his eyes, the touch of his hand upon my shoulder as he called me brother.

I have resigned my commission and will go to Capernaum to see my friend Tyrus. He is now a member of a group who follow the words of Jesus. I have much to learn from him. I write this letter to you at the direction of Jesus, that night in his cell. He told me of your great faith, compassion, and love, as well as your ability to heal. He said you would be a great force in my life if I choose his way.

And I do so choose.

Respectfully,

Marcus Aurelias

To Kathryn, from Joseph of Arimathea.

I have been a secret believer and follower of the Rabbi Jesus for some time. Because I am a high-ranking member of the Jewish Sanhedrin in Jerusalem, I knew first-hand how the council felt about Jesus. They called him a rabble-rouser, apostate, and a grave danger to the Jewish faith. I knew that, if my feelings about Jesus were known, I would be in danger of being removed from the tribunal and my life could be threatened as well. My pride and cowardice caused me to choose safety and maintaining the status quo. I told myself I could be Jesus' eyes and ears and alert him when necessary of the council's plans, especially if they decided to stop his movement and/or punish him.

On the day they decided to arrest Jesus, I was home with a very ill wife, so I did not hear their plans and was not able to alert Jesus. I was devastated and heartbroken when I heard he had been arrested, tortured, and crucified. I felt my breath escape from my body and I fell to the floor. This was my fault! I wasn't there when he needed me.

I soon realized I could no longer hide my devotion to Jesus and his teachings, and I decided I was through being a coward. I stopped to tell my disciple, Nicodemus, then we headed straight to Golgotha, but we were too late—Jesus had just died.

Jesus' mother, Mary Magdalene, Salome, and John the loved one were still at the foot of the cross. We told them why we had come, and joined them in their tears. Then I sent Nicodemus to gather the spices and burial cloth that had been set aside for my death years ago, while I went off to Pilate to claim Jesus' body. While Pilate was surprised that Jesus was already dead, because people being crucified usually take a much longer time to die, he had no problem releasing the body to me, since I was on the Sanhedrin.

When I returned to Golgotha, John, Nicodemus, a kind centurion, and I took Jesus down from the cross and gently laid him across the lap of his mother. The scene that followed, of a mother wailing over the death of her child, will never leave my mind. It seemed to last several hours. Mary was spent. Eventually, she looked up and said, "I am ready."

Nicodemus fetched water and we used some cloths to bathe his body, then wrapped him with spices and the burial cloth. Someone nearby had an empty cart and offered it to move the body. So began the small procession to the garden near Golgotha, to the tomb I had planned to use for myself. John, Nicodemus, the centurion, and I placed Jesus on the stone slab in the tomb and then, saying our last goodbyes, rolled the stone over the mouth of the cave.

Then I went to the council and told them what I had done. They were shocked and angered at my betrayal. There was much discussion about the fact that I had buried him without their permission, and about my role in all of this. I am ordered to appear before the council on the first day of the week to hear what action will be taken against me. Kathryn, I have to tell you: I could care less. For the first time in a long time, I am without fear.

I deeply mourn the death of my beloved friend and teacher. I have learned much and understand that my path is not with the Sanhedrin, but with the followers of Jesus. I have no misgivings or doubts about my path, for I know I am following the words and direction of the Messiah Jesus.

Thank you for your time,

Joseph, proud to be a follower of Jesus the Messiah

Dear Kathryn, from Mary, the mother of James.

After Jesus died and when the Sabbath day was over, Mary Magdalene, Salome, and I headed out for the tomb with spices to complete the burial rituals. We also brought water and some food so we could sit at the site and rest and remember him before we headed back to the city.

The three of us were distraught, discouraged, and fatigued from the events of the past few days. We worried about how we would get the large stone rolled back from the front of the cave; we knew we could not do it. We were hoping there would be some men in the area who might help.

It took us longer than we expected to get there because of our great physical and emotional fatigue. We had no idea what was to happen to those of us that follow Jesus. Was it over? Would one of the disciples assume leadership? Peter showed what a coward he was and most of the other men followed suit. John the beloved was one of the few exceptions; he stood by us at the cross. We will just have to wait and see.

We were shocked when we arrived at the site—the stone was already rolled back! We stood there, wondering who had done it. Then we entered and came to an abrupt stop because the body was gone. All three of us began to cry and call out Jesus' name. Then, suddenly, from the corner of the cave came a voice: "Do not be afraid, for you will soon see Jesus again in Galilee. Tell your friends Jesus has been raised. He is not dead."

We looked at one another and knew by the look on each other's faces that we all had heard the voice. Mary said, "We need to go back to Jerusalem as quickly as we can." We ran as fast as we could, which was not very fast, to reach the others and tell them what we had seen and heard.

When we got there, we were so out of breath we could barely talk. We had not had a chance to eat the food we had brought or even drink the water. The men were patient with us and let us catch our breath and have some nourishment before we began our story.

Once we told the story, they were not quite so solicitous. They called us hysterical women. They began interrogating us and were more concerned about where Jesus' body was and who had taken it. James tried to intercede and said, "My mother does not tell lies." They accused the Romans, the council, and someone even suggested Jewish rebels took it to arouse the people to rebellion.

Finally, Peter was able to quiet the room and said he and John would go see for themselves what had happened. He told everyone to stay in the room till he and John returned. Despite his orders, Mary Magdalene went with them. She is a woman to be reckoned with. Salome and I left to go to her home in Jerusalem, for we were near collapse by that time.

Later that day, Mary Magdalene found us to relate what had happened. John was the first to reach the tomb, since he was the youngest. He saw the stone had been rolled back, but chose to wait for Peter to arrive. They entered the tomb and saw the burial cloth lying on the platform. They finally believed we were telling the truth and went back to tell the rest of the men that the body really was gone. But they still had no idea what we should be doing.

Mary then told us what had happened to her after the men had gone. I will let Mary tell you herself. It was miraculous.

Much love and respect,

Mary, mother of James

Dear Kathryn, from an elated Mary Magdalene.

I am not sure what you have heard or from whom, but I wanted to tell you what happened to me. Mary, Salome, and I had gone back to the tomb to tend to the body of Jesus, but it was gone. We returned to the others in the upper room in the city and told them that the tomb was empty and Jesus' body was gone.

Immediately there was an uproar. They did not believe it and wanted to see for themselves. Peter said he and John would go and see for themselves. Others complained and wanted to go, but he was adamant about the rest of us staying in the room. I ignored him and joined those who were leaving as the discussion continued.

When we arrived, the tomb was still empty. Only the burial cloth was left on the stone platform. The men left quickly to tell the group what we had said was true.

I was still shaken to the core. Not only had they murdered my beloved, they now had stolen his body. I lay down on the platform, wrapping myself in his shroud. My whole body was shaking as I sobbed, gasping for breath.

I did not know how much time had passed when I felt a presence and lifted my head. There were two men, shining like the sun, standing at the end of the platform. In unison, they said, "Woman, why are you weeping?"

I sat up and answered, "Someone has taken my beloved and I do not know where he is." Then a man appeared at the entrance of the cave. I did not know who he was—maybe the gardener, I thought—and he asked why I was weeping. I said, "The body of my Lord is gone. If you took him, please tell me where he is."

The man did not say anything at first, just looked deeply into my eyes, then said, quietly, "Mary, my beloved." Suddenly I recognized him and stood up, running to him. I threw my arms around him, holding him as tightly as I could, and felt his body against mine as he embraced me. There was a live Jesus in my arms! I could scarcely believe it!

He took a deep breath and dropped his arms, stood back, and said, "Mary, you must let me go, as I still have work to do on this earth before I go to my father." He then directed me to go back to his followers and tell them what I had heard, seen, and felt.

I went as quickly as I could, returning to the upper room, and this time they believed. We know there is more to come. Jesus will let us know what our mission is, who he is, and what we are to do next.

With great joy,

Mary

Dear Kathryn, from Claudius Balbus.

I am a centurion in the Roman army. My unit was assigned by Pontius Pilate to guard the tomb of the rebel Jesus of Nazareth. The authorities were afraid his followers would steal the body and claim some sort of miracle. It was not a happy assignment. There were six of us assigned to wait for the body to arrive at the tomb where Pilate had been told the body would be buried. When they arrived, there were only two old men and one young one, followed by a few women. I knew the men would not be able to move the stone. They proceeded with the burial ritual and then began to slowly move the stone, by inches.

None of our detachment offered to help. I do not know why, but I stepped up after a while and helped them move the stone. I had been assigned to the crucifixion as well, so I sensed his friends and family had been through enough. They were very grateful. My fellow soldiers started to hoot and holler like it was a game of sorts. I was embarrassed for them.

When the stone was in place, the group left and I set the rotations for our vigil. Three men on guard at all times with twelve-hour rotation.

Two days later, early in the morning, the women came back to the tomb just as I and two other guards arrived to assume our shift. As the women approached the tomb, the earth suddenly shook. The tremor did not last long, but it dislodged that heavy stone, which rolled away from the tomb. Then an even stranger event followed. Some sort of being appeared, who radiated a blindingly bright white light and announced, "Do not be frightened! Jesus has been raised from the dead. Go now and tell his disciples this news. He will soon be with them in Galilee." The women bowed before this man and paid homage, as if he were royalty. Then they hurried to leave and bring the news to their friends.

We immediately checked the tomb, and it was empty. The six of us were struck dumb for a few minutes. Our assignment was to make sure no one took the body. No one did—it just disappeared! Then this strange being appeared and spoke. All six of us heard and saw the same thing, but none of us had an explanation for it.

Now came the hard part: Myself and two of the other guards went to the chief priests to explain what happened. Each of us swore by the god Zeus that what we said was the truth. They ordered us to wait while they left to decide how to handle the situation. They returned after an hour or so and said all six of us were to swear by Zeus that we fell asleep, and his followers came during the night and stole his body. They instructed me to command the other guards to follow the plan and gave us a good sum of money, to divide among us, in return for lying about what happened.

I knew it would be no problem for the men to lie about the incident, even without the money. But I feel guilty about it. I think I want to learn more about this rabbi. I have heard from some Jewish friends that you are a wise and good woman. I thought you should hear the truth.

May I write to you in the future with questions and concerns about what has happened?

Claudius Balbus

Dear Kathryn, from Cleopas, a follower of Jesus.

I hope you remember me from my visit with you several years ago. You helped with my nervous condition by praying with me and offering sage advice. Since then, I have become a member of the community that follows the Rabbi Jesus. I am not sure you have heard the latest news about him, since it just happened a few days ago.

Jesus was tortured, crucified, died on a cross and has risen from the dead. At first, we could not believe he was still alive, but there are people I trust who validated the truth of it. It all caused me a great deal of fear, anxiety, and stress. I was worried the authorities would come after us. Our group's leaders seemed immobilized by fear and were failing to lead. No one knew what to do. Bartholomew, one of his other followers, was worse off than I was. He could not keep his food down. So, we decided to leave for a few days and go home to our village, which is about a day's walk from Jerusalem.

On the way to Emmaus, we discussed all the things that had happened over the past few days: the last meal we had with Jesus, Judas' betrayal, Jesus' arrest, the crucifixion, the burial, then brothers and sisters from our group seeing the resurrected Jesus, alive and speaking to them. It was all too much to absorb.

About an hour into the walk, we met up with another traveler. He was walking to the village as well. He joined the conversation by asking many questions about what we were describing. It seemed as if he had not heard any of what we were talking about. I said to him, "Are you the only man in Jerusalem that has not heard of these things? Where have you been?"

He responded by quoting lines about the Messiah from the scriptures. It was clear he was a holy man. As we approached the town, he began to veer off in another direction. We urged him to dine with us and spend the night. He was reluctant, but we encouraged him since it was almost night and not safe to be on the road.

Our families were delighted to see us and prepared a feast. We sat down and my father said the blessing. When he was through, and before we started eating, the man stood (for some reason, we had never asked his name), blessed the bread, broke it into pieces, said, "Take this," and handed bread to each one of us at the table.

We had last seen this ritual occur at the Passover meal we shared with Jesus. Bartholomew and I looked at each other and, at once, we knew it was the risen Christ. We realized that, when he was quoting scripture about the Messiah on the road, he was talking about himself. We finished the meal and escorted him to the door when he said he needed to go. As he left, we bowed before him and said, "My lord and my God." He took our hands as we stood, embraced us, and said, "Go, tell the others. We shall meet again." And, at that moment, both of us were free of all fear and anxiety.

We said goodbye to our families, telling them it was important that we get back to Jerusalem as quickly as possible. We took the risk of traveling by night, knowing we would not come to any harm, as we were under the protection of the one with all the power of Yahweh.

Many blessings and thanks again to you,

Cleopas

Dear Kathryn, from John the beloved disciple.

So much has happened these last few months. Jesus had been performing more and more miracles. Crowds that followed him were getting larger and larger, hoping he was the Messiah and become a political leader who would return Israel to self-rule. Talk of insurrection grew. Authorities planted spies among us.

But his message never changed. It was always one of love and service. Most recently, it included urgency: "The hour grows near, when I will be returning to the Father." We did not know what that meant. When we questioned him, he would say, "Soon, all will be revealed."

It was a confusing and unsettling time and I know I was not alone in those feelings. But Jesus would take me aside, assuaging my fears and worries. I do not know why, but Jesus had a special place in his heart for me. He treated me as much-loved younger brother. And I was deeply devoted to him, and loved him with all my being. It often caused resentments among the other men.

After they crucified Jesus, and shortly after he was entombed, he began appearing to us, both disciples and women followers. Initially, he appeared to individuals at the tomb, in the garden of Gethsemane, and on the road. These people reported to us what had happened, but it was very hard to believe them. We knew they believed it, because these people are honest and trustworthy followers of Jesus and would not lie. Were they hallucinating?

We all were confused by the news and still very fearful. No one seemed to know what to do. The day of the crucifixion, Mary Magdalene had given us directions on what had to be done. But Peter still seemed paralyzed with fear and none of the other men were stepping up. The door to the room was locked as we all were terrified the Temple police might be searching for us.

All his followers (except Thomas), men and women alike, regathered on the evening of the first day of the week in the upper room where we had celebrated Passover. The room was very noisy because there was much talking, and even arguing, going on. Suddenly, Jesus appeared in the room. As people realized it, the room became deathly silent. Everyone was staring at him and waiting.

Jesus stood there for what seemed like quite a while. Then he said, "Peace be with you" and showed us his wounds to prove it was he. He then asked for some water and something to eat, I think to prove he was not a spirit. He said the time was short, he soon would be going to be with his Father, and we had much to learn. He instructed us not to leave Jerusalem because somehow he knew that some of the men were planning on leaving to see their families. He then breathed on us and said, "Receive the Holy Spirit. Whoever's sins you forgive are forgiven. Whoever's sins you retain are retained." This was confusing and I am still unsure what it meant—and I was not alone in that feeling.

Jesus was with us for several hours, taking time to speak to some of us individually. There was so much to absorb. I kept thinking I could not measure up to his expectations and then, as if he could read my thoughts, he said, "John, do not be afraid. Be patient and all will be well."

He then disappeared as suddenly as he had appeared. We were all stunned and tangibly felt the absence of his presence in the room. We were all drained of energy, as if it left with Jesus. Jesus continues to meet with us at different times, and that feeling happens each time he leaves.

He says the time is soon coming that he will be going to be with his Father and we will not see him anymore, but he also says, "I will always be with you." More confusion. I am turning to you, knowing you were one of his confidants. I'm hoping you might clarify Jesus' words, as you knew him so well.

Thank you for always being there,

John, the beloved

Dear Kathryn, from Thomas, a disciple of the risen Jesus.

Thank you for your prayers for my twin brother, who was ill. He has been healed and is slowly regaining his strength. I am grateful to all my friends, including you, who prayed him into good health. I was very worried. He was near death and the thought of losing him would be like losing part of myself, but all is well now. I was able to leave him in good hands and I am back in Jerusalem.

I know John wrote you about the appearance of Jesus, but when they told me about it, I could not believe it. It just could not be true! I saw with my own eyes his dead body—though from afar, as I was too much a coward to get close. I heard his mother wailing as they took him down from the cross. No! It cannot be! People do not come back from the dead. It must be the devil working his evil ways—or so I thought.

About a week had passed when I returned to Jerusalem. I met with my spiritual brothers in the same room where we had Passover. They continued to try and convince me they had seen the risen Jesus. I said, "The only thing that would convince me is if I put my fingers in his nail marks and my hand in his side. Only then will I be convinced." There was much discussion about whether I should be allowed to stay with the group because of my disbelief.

Suddenly, Jesus appeared in the room. The door had been locked and yet, there he was. I recognized him immediately. He spoke directly to me: "Thomas, put your finger on my wounds, your hand in my side." I cried out, "Lord, I do believe!" Jesus said, "This is one of your weaknesses. You must learn to trust and become like those who trust without proof."

He continued on with his teachings, as well as using me as an example of how not to behave. I have much to learn. Jesus did approach me privately and relieved me of the guilt I had for not believing. I had not shared that feeling with anyone, but he knew, without me saying anything.

Thank you again for all you do and for who you are.

Thomas

Dear Kathryn, from Peter, disciple to Jesus the Messiah.

It has been several weeks since the risen Messiah began appearing to us. He comes unannounced and is gone before we are aware of it. He has appeared in several different places, even once when some of us were fishing. For some reason I cannot understand, he continues to want me to be the leader of his followers. It does not make any sense to me, since I have so many faults. I denied him—not once, but three times, because I am a coward. I am prideful and arrogant at times, as well as undependable. Yet he insists in his choice of me. I am to be the shepherd and the disciples are the lambs.

I miss my family very much and wish I could go back to just being a husband, father, and fisherman instead of a shepherd.

Jesus' message when he comes to us is to prepare for our mission before he returns to the Father. The message is to live the beatitudes and share all that he has taught us with all nations. I am not sure what that means. When I ask the question, he says, "Be patient, Peter, more will be revealed."

When he is with us, I feel unafraid and strong. When I am alone, I feel weak and fearful. He says the time will come when he will return to his Father and then says, "but I will always be with you." When I question this, his answer is, "The time will come when you will have all understanding."

He has appeared to both his mother Mary and to Mary Magdalene individually, but neither feels comfortable sharing, saying, "It was too personal." I check with them on a regular basis to make sure they are alright. Since Jesus began his visits, they are more than alright—they are euphoric. I wonder what will happen when he finally leaves?

For all I know, Jesus may have appeared to you as well. I know you were a valuable and holy supporter of his work and he spoke of you often, encouraging all of us to take advantage of your wisdom and help. He often says, "Do not forget Kathryn."

Your friend and servant,

Peter

Dear Kathryn, from Anna, follower of Jesus the Christ.

So much has happened in these last forty days. Jesus has returned from the grave and appeared to many of us, many times, in many different places. His appearance is just as he was before his death. He has a need for food and wine and partakes of it alongside us. He takes the bread, blesses it, and says, "Take of this, for it is my body."

While we did not know which particular day was to be his last time with us, he kept reminding us that his time to return to his Father was drawing near. One day, he directed us to meet him on Mount Olivet. All of his disciples who were in the area, men and women alike, were gathered there. As usual, we women provided sustenance for the day.

We did not have to wait long before he appeared. He spoke of his need for us to continue his work, and carry his message to all nations—Jew and Gentile alike. We are to gather in community and live as family, brothers and sisters to each other. When one of us is hurt or in need—whether it is material, emotional, or spiritual—all are responsible. He said it is not just the women who should provide for the community. And he was adamant that women should be respected as equals and treated as such, the same way he treated any woman he encountered in his life and ministry. He said we can learn much from women about love and caring.

He spoke at length about his expectations of us. The words may have been different, but the message is the same as the other times he appeared to teach us. He said we should not just speak his words but live his words. He gave many examples and answered many questions. Then someone asked, "Are you going to restore the kingdom to Israel?" He answered, "It is not time for you to know. Only the Father knows. When I am gone, the Spirit will come upon all of you and you will be my witnesses through all the earth." As he said this, he began to rise off the ground, as if on a cloud, and slowly disappeared into the sky.

I started to weep, as did many of the other women. He was our champion. He often chastised any man he found disrespecting a woman. This was a new concept for us—treating women as equals. What will become of us now? Will the men remember his message about women, or will they return to their old ethics and behaviors? Only time will tell. We all, men and women alike, felt special in his eyes, but the women have a special place in his heart and I know he will not desert us.

His gifts to us as women were self-esteem and the strength to act as valuable people on this earth. We will act with courage while we wait to go be with our Father in heaven.

With deep respect,

Anna

Dear Kathryn, from Matthias, a conflicted disciple of Jesus.

I have just been chosen to take the place once held by Judas Iscariot among the apostles. Last week, Peter announced that it was time to choose a replacement and Barnabas and I were proposed. We both were excited and overwhelmed by the possibility. To be numbered among the twelve apostles is a great honor. Peter invoked the guidance of God, lots were passed out, and shortly thereafter my name was announced by Peter: "Matthias is to be counted with the remaining eleven apostles."

After the initial excitement, with everyone congratulating me and Peter sharing his expectations of me, I began to have doubts and fears about my abilities to do the job. Judas was a master in managing the finances, coordinating activities, seeing to Jesus' well-being and safety. I certainly do not want to follow in his shoes as a traitor, but in all other things he excelled.

The other issue that is bothering me is that, for all of history, my name and the name of Judas could be forever connected. "Matthias, the one who took the place of Judas the traitor." I feel shame in that, but I know the shame is not mine. Can one be guilty by association?

As you can see, I feel very conflicted about this. I followed and loved Jesus from the time I met him, very early in his ministry. I listened, observed, and learned. I became part of his community. I mourned his death, grieved his loss, suffered deeply with the thought of never seeing him again, of losing the dream of a new Kingdom of Israel. But, when I was honored with his presence after he rose from the tomb, hearing his words with new ears, I really learned about his mission of unconditional love and acceptance. He wanted me to be a manifestation of his love and teaching—not just speak his words but be his words. I became even more devoted and more in love with this man called Jesus.

I would have been happy to be part of the 120 disciples, doing what was asked and supporting the true leaders, but now my place is among the chosen few and I do not feel ready or worthy.

Barnabas shows no evidence of being resentful or envious. He has been most loving and kind in his support of me. He offered his knowledge and expertise in areas where I have little or no experience. I think he may feel a sense of relief that it is me and not him. I am sure the Lord has different plans for him, for he has many talents to share.

I have been praying and asking for guidance, and your name came to me in a dream. You have helped so many people, myself included. You are a gift from the Holy Spirit, for which I am truly grateful.

Respectfully, and with much love,

Matthias

Dear Kathryn, from Andrew, an apostle of Jesus.

For the past forty days, Jesus had been with us, instructing us and chiding us when necessary to prepare us for our mission. He told us we were to become witnesses to his birth, his life, his death and resurrection to all the people of the earth.

We were gathered in the upper room to celebrate the feast of Pentecost when suddenly the sky darkened and a gale-force wind swept through the room with a roar. What appeared to be tongues of fire appeared over each of our heads. Once again, we did not know what was happening. After several minutes, we all felt heat rising up through our bodies. Then suddenly, we felt courage, determination, and intense love flow through our bodies. We knew then we were all filled with the Holy Spirit, just as Jesus had predicted.

Jerusalem was filled with pilgrims from near and far to celebrate Pentecost. They saw the sky darken and heard the noise of the wind. Many rushed to gather below the window of our room. Some were shouting out, "What happened? Do you need any help?"

We all went out on the flat roof of the building and the crowd became quiet. Peter spoke first, with such eloquence and passion that people in the group were soon nodding in agreement and shouting, "Amen!" It looked like all the pilgrims understood him, even though he was speaking Aramaic and the people were from Asia, Rome, Judea, Mesopotamia, and many other places. The crowd was a mixture of Jews, converts, Cretans, and Arabs. We all took turns speaking to the crowd, with the same results: They heard their native language, while we were speaking Aramaic. The crowd kept getting larger because more people wondered what was happening.

We had been out on the roof for several hours when the people in the crowd began to shout, "What are we to do?" Peter answered, "Repent and be baptized." At that point, we all left the roof, went into the crowd, and asked them to follow us to the ritual waters that flow by the steps leading up to the Temple. There, we began baptizing all the men and women. During each baptism, we promised people that their sins would be forgiven and they also would receive the gift of the Holy Spirit.

It was late in the day when the crowd dispersed. We returned to the upper room totally exhausted, but also exhilarated. We found the owner of the building had left food and wine for us in the room. We were extremely grateful, for we needed the sustenance. As we talked, we compared numbers and realized that, between all of us, we had baptized about three thousand people!

After we had taken our refreshment, Peter spoke to us. He speaks with a different voice now, one of authority, but with love and kindness. He suggested we all retire to our homes or guest rooms and meet in 24 hours to begin our plans on how to share the word of Jesus the Christ—our active ministry. We need to remember we are the chosen ones and the message should be not just what we say, but who we are.

You have been such a big part of many of our lives, as well a confidant and friend of Jesus. I thought it important that you be kept aware of this momentous occasion. We know we are to baptize in the name of the Father, and the Son, and the Holy Spirit. We will have the power to work miracles, practice the beatitudes, and continue the breaking of the bread and telling the story of Jesus' life. This is our work.

My hope is that you will continue to support us in this ministry. If you need help in any way, feel free to contact me.

Your servant,

Andrew, Apostle to the risen Lord

Dear Kathryn, from your cousin Judith.

You know I have been experiencing difficulty conceiving. Jonah and I have been praying for a miracle for several years. So, we decided to go to Jerusalem for Passover this year and stay for Shavuot, since it is a celebration of the fertility of the crops and fertility is just what we need.

One day we went to Temple for services and then went to find somewhere to have a meal. The town was crowded with Jews from all over the world. It was a cacophony of languages. The streets were so dense it was hard to move through the crowd. Suddenly, the sky became dark and we heard a roaring noise, the sound of a great wind, but nothing was moving. People were standing and looking around, not knowing what was happening. I was holding onto Jonah because I was so frightened.

We were in front of a meeting house, where men had gathered on its flat roof alongside an upper room. One of them raised his hands and said, "Do not be afraid! There is nothing to fear." He had to say it several times before the crowd quieted and settled down.

As he began to speak, the crowd grew in size. We were packed in so tight I thought that if people started to panic there would be many injuries. But the longer he talked, the calmer the crowd got. The man was talking about the Rabbi Jesus. Those of us who live in Judea knew about him, but I am sure few of the foreigners had ever heard of him. And this is the strangest thing I have ever witnessed: The man on the roof was speaking Aramaic, which Jonah and I could understand, but the people in the crowd who did not speak Aramaic could also understand, because somehow they were hearing him speak in their native language!

The man talked about Jesus' life, his miracles, his unconditional love for all people. He said that Jesus knew what was in our hearts and also our needs. He said we should commit ourselves to a new way of living and praying. One by one, other men on the roof took turns sharing their experiences with Jesus. It when on for hours and the crowd was mesmerized. No one left.

Then, "Repent and be baptized!" one of the men on the roof shouted. There was a brief discussion on the roof, then one man told us, "Stay where you are. We will come down to you." We followed the men to the waters that flow into the ritual baths by the Temple steps.

There, we waited in line for a long time, for our turn to be baptized. It was amazing how patient everyone was while we waited our turn. We were all acting as if we were family or friends. We spoke of the messages we'd heard, each in our own native tongue.

Finally, it was my turn. As the water poured over me, I felt an energy course through my body and it brought me to tears.

None of us wanted to leave, even after we were baptized. It turned into an amazing addition to the Pentecost festival. When the men finally left to return to their rooms, the crowd began to disperse. We all kept talking about how each of us heard the same message, but in different languages.

Jonah and I left for home the next day, talking about nothing else. That was two months ago, and I have missed two of my bleeding times since then. I am overjoyed and can hardly believe it is happening. Jesus did know what was in our hearts, without us speaking a word. I am with child!

I will be going to the midwife soon to verify that I am truly pregnant, but I really do not need it. I know when my mother hears the news she will want me to go to her. When that is done, then Jonah and I will tell the good news to all my family and friends.

Your believer in Jesus,

Judith

Dear Kathryn, from Mary of Magdala.

It has been about twelve weeks since my Lord Jesus left this earth to return to his Father. I miss him every minute of every day. I long to feel his touch, see his smile, and hear his voice. But, before he left this earth, he blessed us with his Holy Spirit and I feel that presence on a daily basis. I have a fire burning within me to share his message and be an example of his love, forgiveness, compassion, acceptance, and generosity. There are times I am even a conduit of his power to heal—and I do not know who is more surprised, the one healed or me.

Shortly after Jesus returned to the Father, Peter asked me to speak with him in private. He acknowledged the importance of the women followers—all we had done while Jesus was alive, our courage when many of the men deserted him, and how we continue to do his work since his ascension.

We have many Jewish and Gentile converts and not enough apostles to support and guide them on their path as new Christians—this is the name the public has given to those of us who are followers of Jesus. Peter said he has been praying about the problem and felt directed to ask me to join him in his position as co-leader of the apostles. He recognized that I had a personal and deep love for Jesus, without the benefits of a conjugal relationship. Because of this, he realized I could bring a different perspective on how we should behave and teach his message.

We called the followers together and broke bread, prayed the Our Father, and then asked the group to close their eyes, take deep, relaxing breaths, and listen to the news we were about to share. We each spoke for about ten minutes about what our mission would be as equal co-leaders. After we finished speaking, we remained silent for a few more minutes, then asked them to open their eyes and share their thoughts about our proposal. Instead of speaking, the women stood and began smiling and dancing in place, then the men began to stand. Everyone was applauding and hugging one another. It was wonderful. Without any discussion, this consensus was reached—because each of us had been infused with the Spirit.

From this time forward, any woman or man sharing the message and practicing the teachings of Jesus will be known as an Apostle and become a part of the governing group. Newcomers will have to present themselves to this group of apostles for approval.

We all certainly experienced the Spirit in the room. We all felt the love and acceptance of one another. We cannot see into the future, but, if we can continue to act as one, as sisters and brothers in Christ, we have nothing to fear.

With deep regard for all you do,

Mary of Magdala

Dear Kathryn, from Peter, servant of Jesus the Christ.

It has been almost a year since Our Lord was crucified and rose from the dead. Jesus did direct me to keep you informed of the work we are doing to spread his message and, when troubled or anxious, to seek out your gifts and wisdom. So, here is an update.

The apostles and disciples have gone out in pairs, teaching, working miracles, feeding the poor, and healing the sick. Many people, from all walks of life and different parts of the country, have been converted to the Way, even some of the priests from the council.

We meet as a group on a regular basis, including the women who were among the early followers of Jesus. We discuss any problems, make future plans, and give out assignments. We begin each meeting with the breaking of the bread and prayers. Decisions are made only after lengthy discussions and then through consensus of the attendees.

The new followers, as well, meet daily in the morning for prayers and the breaking of the bread as a way to start the day with the teachings of Jesus uppermost in their minds.

At the last leadership meeting, the need for more disciples was raised. We are not able to meet all the temporal needs of our new followers since we have grown tenfold. Some of these people are without shelter, food, or money. Yet, there are others who joined us who have sold their homes and belongings and turned the money over to us to be divided among those in need. We need people with talent and tact to disperse the money in an equitable, nonjudgmental way. And, honestly, we were a bit wary of who we picked because of our experience with Judas.

After much discussion, we agreed that Stephen should take the lead on this project. He accepted, with one condition: He wanted Veronica as part of the team because of her experience with running a business and her own household, as well as being an outstanding example of Jesus' teachings.

Now for the not-so-good news. We Christians, since that is what the nonbelievers have chosen to call us—and we proudly accept that title—are being severely persecuted, even unto death. Devout Jews accuse us of false teachings, blasphemy, and working miracles in league with the evil one. They accuse us of no longer being Jews because we choose not to follow the rules related to food, circumcision, ritual cleanliness, and honoring the Sabbath according to their teachings. This is very strange, because all of us, men and women, who were with Jesus during his lifetime think of ourselves as observant Jews. We learned from him what it meant to be a good and holy Jew.

The Sanhedrin has commissioned a devout young Jew named Saul to hunt us down and to punish and kill us if we choose not to renounce Jesus' teachings. He and a group of Temple police are relentless in their search for any of our community. He boasts of how many Christians he has captured and that it is his mission to eradicate this unholy sect, which he says is corrupting the Jewish religion. Nothing is further from the truth.

Stephen, our deacon, had been preaching the Way and was captured and tried before the council. They demanded he renounce his teachings and he refused. So, Stephen was stoned to death, and to the very end he refused to denounce the Lord.

Jesus' teaching of peace, love, and the Beatitudes were words Stephen lived by.

Blessed are the poor in spirit, for theirs is the kingdom of heaven.

Blessed are they who mourn, for they shall be comforted.

Blessed are the meek, for they shall inherit the earth.

Blessed are they who hunger and thirst for righteousness, for they will be satisfied.

Blessed are the merciful, for they shall obtain mercy.

Blessed are the pure of heart, for they shall see God.

Blessed are the peace makers, for they shall be called children of God.

Blessed are those persecuted for the sake of righteousness, for theirs is the kingdom of God.

These are the words we must not just preach, but live by, every day, no matter what the cost.

We were also instructed to teach all nations, so please pray for more men and women who are willing to give up family and home to join our mission. My family has done just that; they have come to believe that, in giving me up and living the life that Jesus taught them, they are the message by example. I try to get home at least once a month and do miss them very much, but they are very supportive of our work.

I know not what the future holds, but I know I do not need to know. That I also have learned from Jesus. I trust his Spirit is always with us and we just have to be open to that guidance. We are finite human beings and will make mistakes, but I believe, since our intentions are holy, we have nothing to fear. We will learn from those mistakes and go forward as Jesus taught us to do.

I pray for your good health and the safety of our brethren. I hope you will add that to your prayers as well.

Sincerely,

Peter

CPSIA information can be obtained
at www.ICGtesting.com
Printed in the USA
BVHW032111241120
594161BV00009B/85